Book One
DUNGEONS & DRAGON DATING

Virginia McClain

Crimson Fox
PUBLISHING

Published by Crimson Fox Publishing
Turner, Oregon - USA

ISBN: 978-1-963870-09-1

To Artemis,
This is the first book I've written without you,
I hope it doesn't suck.

Chapter One
Assemble the Party

Kiara ignored the soft sunlight streaming through the large open windows—she ignored the cool spring breeze, lightly scented with flowers she didn't know the names of—and she doggedly ignored the quiet rasping breaths of her best friend coming from across the room. Instead, she focused on the slow flip of the card between her fingers. The motion was so familiar to her that she could probably do it in her sleep without any trouble, but if she just kept her mind on the soft *thwap thwap* of the card turning over each of her fingers and back again, maybe she could pretend that Estvalyn hadn't been in a healing coma for the past three days. Maybe she could imagine that the healers hadn't spent the morning discussing options if Estvalyn didn't recover the full use of her legs. Maybe she could even pretend that the whole thing hadn't been her fault.

The ace of hearts between her fingers caught fire and turned immediately to ash.

"Well, that's not a good sign," rasped a voice across the room.

Kiara's head shot up."You're awake!"

Kiara had completely failed to keep the relief out of her voice. She had also jumped to her feet and launched herself to the side of the low healing bed.

"And *you*," Estvalyn chided from the bed, not even trying to sit up yet, "have been brooding by my bedside for... how many days now?"

"Three," Kiara replied. "The healers had to put you under so that your body could absorb the spells they wove without any interference."

"I figured as much." Estvalyn coughed. Kiara did her best not to wince, but she must have failed because Estvalyn glared at her. "You know this isn't your fault, Ki."

"In what realm is this *not* my fault, Est? I threw the fireball that caught you in its blast!"

"And do you remember *why* you threw that fireball in the first place?"

Kiara looked away and frowned at the very clean, very polished wooden floor.

"I am quite certain the hydra that was about to bite me in *half*," Est continued with more than a little exasperation in her voice, "would have killed me outright, with no chance of a healing in there at all. So, forgive me if I don't hold it against you that I was singed a bit by the fireball that made the thrice cursed monster drop me and allowed us all to escape."

After a lengthy pause—during which Kiara *wanted* to list the number of things she could have done that would

NOT have turned her best friend into crispy fried druid, but heroically refrained—Est spoke again.

"That is, I hope we all escaped. We did, right? Cause you look like you've been brooding, but you don't look like you've been mourning, and if anyone actually died then—"

"We got out. All of us. Or ninety percent of us anyway. I'm not sure you count as a hundred percent out."

Estvalyn chuckled, which led to another coughing fit. Kiara winced again as she watched her short, plump, burgundy-skinned best friend wrack with each cough.

"Look," Est continued, once she'd regained her breath, "I knew what I was getting into when I tried to commune with that damned thing, but we were swiftly running out of options and I figured, at the very least, I'd create an opening for the rest of you to get out of that damned cavern."

"Yeah, well, that worked, I suppose. But you should have known I wasn't about to leave you behind."

"You're a very good best friend."

Kiara laughed in self-deprecation. "Never abandon the healer. That's Dungeoning 101, really."

"Then you're a terrible best friend and a mildly competent adventurer," Est corrected.

"I'm a formidable adventurer, thank you *very* much!"

"Really?" Est chided. "I heard you lit your best friend on fire after she'd already gotten her back broken by a hydra?"

"EST!"

"I'm just teasing. Ydan's tits, you're excitable today."

Kiara laughed, immediately felt like crying, and decided to sit on the small stool that had been placed next to the foot of Estvalyn's bed before her legs gave out on her.

"I'm just saying," Est continued after a moment, "that despite the way you're beating yourself up over the whole thing, you actually saved my life back there. So, I guess we're even now."

"Even? Not remotely close, Est. Lighting you on fire as an alternative to letting you get bisected by a rampaging hydra does NOT make us even."

"No? Come on. I saved your life, you saved mine. We're square."

"You are not getting out of a life debt that easily, Estvalyn Stormvale. Now stop."

"Ugh, I hate that we're even keeping tabs on this, Ki. You know that, right? Friends don't keep track of who saved whose ass. They just always save each other's asses and move on with their day."

"You saved my ass before we even knew each other's names, and I am forever indebted to you."

"You cannot be *forever* indebted to me. I refuse. You have saved my ass countless times now, not even including this latest one. We're best friends *and* part of a team, and you have *got* to let this go."

"Nope. Not letting it go until my debt is repaid."

Estvalyn growled and Kiara wondered if she was about to call on her bear form, but just then the healers bustled into the room to do healer things and to consult with Estvalyn on her own assessment of the damage. So for a while Kiara had to be content with quietly brooding in the corner while a lot of words she didn't understand got bandied about and everyone looked very seriously at Estvalyn's legs.

Kiara did not like the way they were looking at Estvalyn's legs AT ALL. She knew that the hydra had come very close to biting her friend in half. It was the reason she'd been desperate enough to risk casting the fireball that had burned away half her best friend's skin and filled her lungs with so much smoke she was still coughing even after three days in a healing coma. She hadn't let herself think about what all of that might mean until their wizard had portalled them back to Dryvenvale, and Kiara had handed Estvalyn's barely breathing body over to the Guild's best healers. Since then, she'd thought of little else. Healing magic could work wonders, she knew—just looking at Est's healed skin, free of any trace of scarring, was proof of that—but there were some things no amount of magic could overcome, and (from what little she understood of Estvalyn's various rants attempting to keep her team intact during missions) severed spines were one of them. But Kiara didn't say anything until all of the healers had bustled out again and Estvalyn was staring quietly out the nearest window that provided a decent view of the city proper.

"Now who's brooding?" she teased, sitting down at the foot of the bed once more.

"Definitely me," Est admitted, a smile not quite reaching her eyes.

"Do I even want to know why?"

"Probably not, but I'll tell you if you'll stop bugging me about this whole life debt thing."

"No deal."

"How about I make a different deal with you? What if I ask a very important favor of you and in exchange for you doing that favor, you consider the life debt paid?"

Kiara just eyed the druid in front of her for a moment. Est seemed very serious, which was rare enough; she also seemed a bit haunted, which was, frankly, unheard of for the petite demonborn.

"Anything," she replied emphatically.

"You promise?" Est asked, her face still devoid of its usual vivid expressions and mischief. "You'll do whatever I ask?"

"Yes. If you think it's an even trade for saving my life, then yes."

"Oh, it's an even trade, but... you're not going to like it," Est warned.

"Fine, so I won't like it. I probably shouldn't, since it's, ya know, paying a debt and all. But you have my word. Name the task and I'll do it."

Est rolled her eyes, and a bit of her usual fire returned to her voice. "Yes, yes, you'd never agree to it if you didn't think it was penance for needing me to save your ass to begin with, I get it."

"That is NOT—"

"So, your penance, dear debtor, is this." Est was clearly in no mood for Kiara's usual excuses. She didn't say anything else, but she produced a single slip of parchment that was practically dripping in brightly colored hearts and decorative script.

Kiara took the piece of parchment as though it might bite her and read the words on it with a dawning sense of horror.

Dragon Dating

Need a little luck to find the romance you've been missing in your life? Our top secret formula is guaranteed to find you the perfect soul mate! The luck of the Dragon and a sense of adventure is all you need to find the special someone who compliments the real you perfectly. Come to our Grand Opening for a free trial!

Kiara couldn't speak for a full minute. Then she looked up into her best friend's eyes to find all their usual mischief returned.

"No, Est, no. You did not."

"Oh, but I did."

"When did you even get this? You've been in a healing coma for three days!"

"I found that flyer before we even left for the Great Chasm."

"But it says the 'Grand Opening' is tomorrow!"

"So it does."

"I swear to ALL the gods, Est, if you let yourself get bitten in half by a fucking hydra just to get me to go on a date—"

"I'd be the greatest best friend in the history of time?"

"I'll kill you."

"That would *not* repay your life debt, Ki. Quite the opposite."

"But A MATCHMAKING SERVICE? Come on! I refuse. You have to pick something better, Est. Something more important. You know I don't date. You can't just—"

"Kiara Mefysta, you swore to do whatever favor I asked of you, and I could have asked you to simply accept that you'd already paid your debt to me by saving my life a hundred times. Instead, you get to play the brooding martyr and go on a date you don't want, through a matchmaking service you're sure to find distasteful, to find a partner that you've sworn you'll never need. Because 'you're not built for love,' or whatever lie you keep telling yourself—even though you've been in love before, and used to enjoy dating back before that awful woman destroyed your heart."

"This is ridiculous, Est. Not everyone needs romantic love to be happy. You've said that yourself, and—"

Est didn't even let her finish her objection, cutting her off as if they'd had this argument a dozen times. Because they had.

"Of course not everyone needs romantic love to be happy! I would never have done this to Kyle, who is clearly very content without any romantic partners and who will live a wonderful, fulfilling life without ever having a single romantic entanglement if everyone would just leave him in peace. But I'm not talking about Kyle, or anyone else, Ki. I'm talking about *you*."

"I am perfectly hap—"

"Do not lie to me, Kiara Mefysta. I'm tired. I'm tired of watching you mope in between jobs because you have no one to share your treasure with. I'm tired of watching you wistfully looking at happy couples walking by in the street. And, yes, my recent brush with death has made me sentimental. So I'm asking you to go on a date. But don't worry, it's run by a dragon so it can't be *that* bad, and I've already filled out all the forms for you. I know you hate paperwork."

Kiara was so frustrated she was almost shouting when she said, "That's not the—"

"I might never walk on my own two legs again, Ki." Est's voice was so quiet it cut through Kiara's objections like a fireball through a gelatinous cube.

Kiara's mouth snapped shut.

"And while that's very far from the end of the world," Est continued, wiping at the corners of her eyes, "I get to feel sad about it for a little while. And the least you can do to repay the *stupid* debt you don't *actually* owe me is go on one little date and then tell me all about it after, ok?"

Kiara couldn't speak without her voice breaking, so she simply nodded, and swallowed, then swallowed again, and when she thought she could finally manage it without crying, she said, "Yeah, you're right. I can do that."

L YRA STARED BLANKLY at the sun-dappled couches and plush rugs that filled the café beyond the counter and unscrewed one more jar of toffees, handed them to Sylvan, and sighed. Even the smell of fresh coffee, pastries, and woodsmoke couldn't pull her out of the mood she'd slid into after Lady Aster had come by this morning.

"What's that for?" Sylvan asked.

"The jar on the counter," Lyra replied vaguely, already reaching for a bag of beans to refill the grinder.

"Not the toffees, ya goon. The sighing."

Lyra frowned at the bag of beans she'd begun to unlace and then turned so that she frowned at Sylvan. Her best friend returned the frown, unfazed.

"You heard Lady Aster this morning," Lyra said, trying to keep the exasperation out of her voice. "The rent's going up *again* next month."

"So? I thought business was booming. Weren't you the one crowing about how many customers the new Mage Guild campus was bringing in this month? We aren't going out of business, are we?"

"No, no! Of course not. Og's balls, it's not the end of the world. It's just…"

"Just what?" Syl asked, too perceptive as always.

"Just… the way this neighborhood is going, eventually rent is going to outstrip our earnings, and we'll either have to move to a cheaper location or shut our doors. I *really* wish I could just afford to buy this place."

"Would Lady Aster even sell it to you?" Syl asked, shifting her attention to sorting the toffees nicely into the pretty container on the counter that made it easy to lure patrons into a last–second purchase.

"She leads with an offer to let me buy the place every time she tells us about a rent increase. Were you even listening?"

Sylvan shrugged. "Honestly, no. Once she gets beyond her vague compliments about my fur and my figure, I tend to stop listening."

"Ha! Well, that's fair enough. I'm surprised you even listen to those. It seems weird to me that she makes the same compliments every single time. Unless she's flirting. Do you think she's flirting?"

Sylvan let out a bellowing laugh that shook the whole counter and Lyra smiled at the sound.

"I've learned that anyone who feels the need to point out that I have *fur* every time they see me is generally not actually interested in flirting, no matter how many compliments they may hide the observation under. Anyway, stop trying to distract me. I was about to say that it's not like I could afford to help you buy this place even if I wanted to."

"I know that—hence the sighing."

"Couldn't you dance your way into the extra money?"

"I wish! If I could get enough free time to perform more than once in a blue moon I wouldn't worry so much about the rent hikes, but even when you close up for me that still leaves me doing accounting until supper time and... ugh, I just don't have the energy for more than one or two practice sessions a week anymore."

"And that's not enough for regular performances?"

Lyra actually laughed at that. "I mean, maybe for a more casual troupe, but not for the Night Guild. And performing for anyone else wouldn't pay enough to be worth it."

"But you love it."

"Yeah, but if it can't pay at least *some* of the bills…" Lyra sighed again.

"What you need," Sylvan announced loudly while casually popping scones into the industrial oven in the back room, making Lyra glad that there were no customers lingering after this morning's initial rush, "is a partner."

"Of course, I do! That's what I'm talking about! But you just said you can't afford to split the cost with me and who else do I know who'd have any reason to want to invest in this place?"

"Not a *business* partner, Ly," Syl said, dusting excess flour from her hands.

"Not this again," Lyra muttered. "I already have a roommate to help cover rent. My problems are financial, not social. You keep talking as if a romantic partner will somehow solve my problems instead of just creating a dozen new ones. I don't need another person who wants to spend time with me, Syl. I have too little time and energy as it is. What I need is a business partner."

"No, I'm serious. You have tons of friends, plenty of folks you can unwind with after a long day, but you don't make time to even see them anymore and you refuse to share your burdens with anyone, Ly. You take too much on yourself, and if you'd just—"

The bell above the entrance rang and both Lyra and Syl shuffled into their usual places for customers. But after a moment, when no one appeared on the other side of the counter, Lyra glanced at her best-friend-turned-employee.

"Did you check the wards this morning?" she asked.

Syl only nodded, her giant mane bobbing along with her furred snout.

Lyra was about to step out from behind the counter in order to check the wards again, or at least startle whoever had managed to keep their invisibility spell in place, (though how anyone had managed to slip a spell past the Guild-sanctioned wards Lyra had commissioned only a month ago was a mystery she did NOT feel like solving) when a tiny cough directed her attention downwards.

She still couldn't see anything though. The counter was blocking her view of the floor and—

A few *fwip-fwips* sounded on the far side of the counter, and then the tiniest dragon that Lyra had ever seen plopped itself onto the wooden boards across which Lyra had been leaning a moment before. She didn't even have a chance to take a breath before the tauryn behind her exploded.

"OH MY GODS THAT IS THE MOST ADOR- ABLE CREATURE I'VE EVER SEEN, LY! CAN WE KEEP IT?!?!?"

Lyra glanced over her shoulder and was astounded to see her six-foot, seven-inch tauryn best friend chewing the tips of her furry fingers in what was presumably an attempt to stop herself from scooping up the tiny dragon, cuddling it close, and naming it George.

"Um... Maybe we should let the dragon introduce themself first? Before they decide to just light us on fire for considering kidnapping them?"

A tiny peep from the little green and purple creature, no taller than Lyra's hand, made Lyra return her attention to them.

She thought they were smiling, and she hoped that sound had been a laugh.

"Humans. Always so amusing," the little creature said in a voice that, though high, seemed much deeper than should have been possible for someone only a few inches tall.

"I can only imagine," Lyra agreed, returning the smile.

She wasn't sure how she felt about the little dragon's comment—it was pretty condescending—but considering how long dragons lived compared to everyone else, she wasn't convinced the dragon had *meant* to be insulting. Sometimes the really long-lived peoples of Tyrlan struggled to treat everyone else like people. She was at least reassured that the dragon seemed to be lumping Syl and Ly into the same category.

"How can we help you, friend?" she asked, keeping her customer service smile firmly in place.

"Was hoping we could help each other!" the little dragon chimed. "Have a business proposition for you."

Lyra's smile grew even wider than Sylvan's at that statement. Dragons were supernaturally lucky creatures, regardless of what they drew their power from. Luck dragons were, of course, the masters of luck, good or bad. But no matter what a dragon hoarded for their power, they always had some mastery of luck itself, and a little luck was just what Lyra needed if she was going to stop worrying about every rent payment and start letting her business flourish.

Perhaps this little dragon was offering her just the partnership she'd been looking for.

Chapter Two
First Encounter

YRA WIPED HER palms on her skirts one more time and shook out her wrists. The windows outside the café were dark already, and they'd closed the shutters and flipped the sign over an hour ago. It was still full of all of her favorite smells: coffee, pastries, woodsmoke, and now the fresh lemon-water that she and Syl used to wipe down all the counters.

None of which stopped her hands from trembling.

"You nervous?" asked Syl from where she stood behind the counter. She had offered to finish closing up while Lyra played guinea pig.

"Remind me why I'm doing this again?"

"Because you need the little dragon to help pay our rent, and they insisted you had to test out the service or else they'd find somewhere else? Also, you said it would be unethical to subject your café customers to a matchmaking service that you know nothing about."

"Right. And why aren't I making you do this instead?" she asked, as if that was actually an option.

"One, because you don't pay me enough to test out matchmaking services off the clock. Two, because the little dragon insisted that *you* had to test it, and three, because I already have enough partners and it would be unethical of me to pretend I was looking for a relationship when I'm not."

"But I'm not looking for a relationship either," Lyra replied, and then cringed at how close that had sounded to whining.

"Yeah, but if things go well you're not going to have to explain to five other people why you entered into a new relationship without checking with them first."

Lyra turned to blink at Syl.

"Five? I thought it was seven?"

"Wasn't working for Pearlyn or Verring anymore so they moved on."

"Huh, ok, but when did—"

"Ly, are you stalling?"

"Why would I be stalling?" Lyra said, keeping her voice as neutral as she could. "This isn't a real date, only a test run."

"Right," agreed Syl, as she wiped down the counter. "Which is why you look like you're about to climb onto a trapeze with a partner you don't trust."

"That's ridiculous, Syl. I would never attempt trapeze with a partner I didn't trust."

"You said you didn't trust Kyle the first time."

"No, I said I wasn't sure he'd care if I died, not that I didn't trust him to catch me."

"How is that different exactly?"

"He'd have to want me dead to—look, can we stick to the topic at hand here?"

"I thought you wanted to stall!"

"Obviously. But it's not helping!"

"Do you trust the dragon?" Syl asked, finally putting the dish cloth and her hands on the counter and looking Lyra dead in the eyes.

Lyra just barely stopped herself from glaring at her best friend. The little love dragon was still setting up shop, and Lyra didn't think the thin wooden door to the broom cupboard would actually be enough to keep a dragon from hearing everything they said, especially now that their last customers had all gone home and there was no more chatter to cover their conversation. But she and Syl had already talked about this, so she didn't have to say much.

"I mean, that's kind of the point of this whole exercise, isn't it?" Lyra said, choosing her words carefully.

"Right. You're testing the system to make sure that your customers are getting a worthwhile service when they sign up."

"A SAFE, worthwhile service. It would be unethical if one of us didn't test it. Even if the little dragon hadn't insisted, I really shouldn't let a matchmaking service make use of our space—and help pay our rent—if I don't know that it's an ethical one."

And the help with rent is too big a plus not to give this a shot, whether I trust the dragon or not, she carefully refrained from saying out loud. Syl knew it anyway; it didn't need to be said. Frankly, Lyra was still surprised by how much rent the little dragon had been willing to pay for such a tiny portion of the café. More than a third of their monthly costs! Lyra had tried to insist that Auryl take up more space, but the little love dragon had insisted that the broom cupboard was all they needed. And since Lyra had more than one cupboard to store brooms and toilet paper in, she wasn't about to complain on that front.

"So, you basically have no choice," Syl said, with a furry smirk.

Being told she had no choice made Lyra want to scream, but it wasn't true. She *did* have a choice, she just didn't particularly like either option.

It wasn't like she'd sworn off dating or anything; it was just that… well, her last two attempts at romance had gone up in flames so fast she hadn't even been able to smell the smoke before she was engulfed in fire.

"It's just one date," she muttered, shaking out her wrists again.

"Could be more, though," Syl prodded, waggling her eyebrows suggestively. "Could be someone special."

Lyra barked out a laugh that sounded hollow even to her own ears.

"Yeah. Right. I'm a bit too broken for 'somebody special,' but one date can't hurt, right?"

The face that Sylvan was making on the other side of the counter when Lyra glanced over her shoulder was not a reassuring one. But even as Syl started talking again, most likely to object to Lyra referring to herself as broken, Lyra shook out her shoulders and her wrists and decided to treat the whole thing as a complicated aerial sequence: potentially dangerous, but best approached with respectful confidence.

"Ly… you—"

"Nope, too late! Into the broom cupboard!"

And with that, she grabbed the handle and opened the door to the tiny closet that Auryl, the love dragon, had taken over a few hours earlier.

Kiara almost turned away with a sigh of relief when she saw the "Closed" sign hanging over the door to "The Right Place" café. She'd walked the surprisingly short distance from her room at the Guild hall, through the old fish market turned bustling shopping district, and quickly arrived at the cozy-looking wood and glass facade to a café that she had somehow never visited before. But just as she began to turn away from the cute, closed café, a shining sign flashed out from just to the left of the door, catching her attention:

Dragon Dating: Famous Magical Matchmaking Services! OPEN!

She blinked at the sign that she was fairly certain hadn't been there a moment earlier, and considered turning around anyway. She could always tell Est that the café had been closed. Maybe pretend she'd not noticed the other sign. Then the sign flashed again, neon shining bright enough to almost hurt her eyes.

Come on in, Mage Mefysta! Your future awaits!

That made Kiara's spine tingle in a way that generally warned her of an unseen attack. The fingers of her left hand twitched and she barely noticed as she automatically started flicking her favorite playing card between her knuckles. She stared at the sign, considering whether she'd be forgiven for walking away and explaining to Est that the whole thing had felt like a trap.

You promised your best friend, the sign flashed. *Do your promises really mean so little, fire mage?*

"What the hells?" Kiara muttered.

The sign was getting a bit *too* personal now, which did nothing to reduce her concern about the whole thing being a trap. On the other hand, it *did* pique her curiosity about the magic that ran this place… and that was enough to get her to open the door.

She was almost disappointed to find that stepping through the door to the matchmaking service simply deposited her in the entrance to the café. She'd half expected the door to portal her somewhere across the continent. The café smelled of coffee, pastries, wood fire, and some sort of citrus, an odd but pleasant mix that fit perfectly with the plush leather chairs and sofas that dotted the small wooden space. As Kiara scanned the room, she noticed a tall, broad shouldered and shapely tauryn woman dressed in a fitted pink shirt and black leggings. The tauryn was standing behind the café counter, cleaning mugs with a cloth. She looked up when the bell jangled.

"We're clo—" The tauryn quirked an eyebrow. "Are you here for Dragon Dating?" she asked instead.

"I was under the impression it was the grand opening and… my friend told me she filled out the paperwork for me, but… am I in the right place?"

The tauryn laughed loudly at that, and only then did Kiara remember the name of the café on the sign outside.

"Ah, yes, sorry, you must get that a lot."

The tauryn nodded but seemed to be schooling her features into something less amused.

"We do, but it never gets old. Sorry. Um, I believe that Auryl, that's the dragon, is waiting for you just past that door."

The tauryn woman, who Kiara could now see wore a small brass name tag that read "Sylvan," gestured towards a rather small door that Kiara would have sworn was a broom cupboard if it hadn't had a very large heart-shaped sign centered on it that read *Dragon Dating: Matches Made with a Dragon's Own Luck.*

"Right. I... guess I'll just head in there then."

Kiara hated that she was already stumbling over her words when the date hadn't even started yet, but she swallowed her irritation and strode toward the door. She flicked away her playing card and adjusted the sleeves of her greatcoat even as she pulled the knob open. As she headed inside, she thought she heard a low whistle behind her, followed by a muttered, "Damn, that dragon got her type down 100%. I might have to sign up for that service after all." But Kiara was too focused on the room ahead of her to pay much attention to the words.

K IARA WAS IMMEDIATELY enveloped by darkness and the smell of coffee beans.

"Well, this is... cozy," she said, as she shuffled inside the closet and pulled the door shut behind her while her eyes adjusted to the lack of light.

The cupboard wasn't as tiny as she'd suspected it would be from the outside. It was at least as deep as she was tall, and she was not a short woman. Yet the space was so narrow that she suspected that the tauryn woman behind the counter would need to turn sideways to make it past the door. Still, despite Kiara being on the curvy end of the spectrum for a half-elf, she had no trouble walking between the empty shelves, though she could feel her leather greatcoat dodging shelf corners and partially exposed nails as she made her way to the far side of the cupboard.

Est had tried to dissuade her from wearing the greatcoat, but Kiara had insisted on it for two reasons. One, she'd enchanted it to the nine hells and it was worth more than her entire house at this point. Leaving it behind was just inviting someone to steal it. And two, it was what she always wore; just because her best friend had badgered her into using a dating service didn't mean she was going to pretend to be something she wasn't.

She *was* wearing one of her nicer tunics, with a lowish neckline, her favorite leather pants, and her stilettoed leather boots (also spelled to the nine hells and back) underneath the greatcoat, but that was as much dressing up as she was willing to attempt.

A faint glow came from the far side of the cupboard, which was enticing simply because there was no other light in the cupboard to speak of. Kiara had long ago stopped being nervous entering small dark spaces containing unknown threats. You didn't make it very long as an adventuring battle mage otherwise, and Kiara had spent more than half her life as one. She didn't hesitate to approach the mysterious light on the far side of the cupboard.

She was unsurprised to find a dragon beside the mysterious light, but she was a bit shocked at how tiny the creature was.

"Hello! Auryl, was it?" she said as she got closer. "I apologize if I'm trespassing, but I was under the impression that this was where I'm meant to be." It never paid to be rude to a dragon, no matter how small it was, a lesson that Kiara had learned hard and fast as a much younger woman.

"Auryl yes. Sylvan told you?"

The tiny voice that cheeped from the dragon no bigger than her hand was still deeper than she would have expected from a creature so small, but she nodded to it, and was grateful that it was standing on a shelf that was just about eye level. The tiny dragon was settled beside a full-length mirror that took up the majority of the back wall of the cupboard. The mirror appeared to be the source of the mysterious glow, although there *were* a few fairy lights strung along the shelves nearby as well. Kiara frowned at those, but did not comment. Apparently, the tiny dragon's overlarge eyes didn't miss much though.

"They are friends, not captives," the little dragon assured her.

Kiara smiled and hoped that the dragon was telling the truth. Dragons were not known for their benevolence, and most of the fairy lights Kiara had ever seen were prisons for fae that had crossed the wrong dragon. Still, Kiara decided to give this little one the benefit of the doubt.

"Grand opening. Big event. Faeries doing favor," it cheeped.

"Right," Kiara replied, trying to keep the skepticism from her voice. "I had rather expected a big event like a grand opening to have more people."

"Ah, but only need two people for matchmaking, no?"

Kiara gave a nervous laugh and nodded. "I suppose so."

"Future mate is already across the portal. You ready?"

Kiara sighed and flicked her playing card across her knuckles. She hadn't even realized she'd brought it out again. She was half tempted to ask the little dragon why it was speaking like a human child, but decided it wasn't worth the risk. Besides, she'd met dragons using stranger manners of speech for no reason beyond that it amused them. Why should this dragon be any different?

"Must agree to terms of spell before begin, yes?"

Kiara sucked in a breath. She wasn't sure what she'd been expecting exactly. Of course a dragon matchmaking service was likely to use *some* amount of magic; she had simply assumed it would be the more passive kind. Not a magical contract.

"If helps, future mate already agreed."

Kiara snorted; just because whatever poor woman this dragon had conned into matching with her had agreed to the terms didn't mean that she would. What were the odds that the other woman was even a mage? Still, there was no use worrying about that until she heard the terms herself, so she just smiled and gestured for Auryl to continue.

"A soul to catch, a love to find, moments of peril will soon unwind hearts too closed and thoughts too bound. I give my consent with arms unbound."

"Really? You're rhyming unbound with bound?" Kiara asked, slightly bewildered by the child-like spell contract.

"Not critique. Repeat," the little dragon grumbled.

Kiara thought over the words for a moment. She hit on one problem almost immediately.

"Moments of peril? In a dating service? Really?"

"Is metaphor."

"Doesn't sound like a metaphor."

"You afraid, battle mage?"

Kiara thought about that. It was perfectly reasonable to be afraid of peril. For all that she had been an adventurer for almost twenty years, she still felt fear before the worst parts of the job—and that was for the best. Fear kept you alive. So, she answered honestly.

"Yep. I'm afraid."

She didn't mention that it wasn't the peril that scared her.

"You gonna give up then?" asked Auryl, with one scaly eyebrow raised.

"Nope. If nothing else, you've already tricked some poor woman into whatever perils lie ahead and I'd bet my greatcoat that unless I go in there after her she'll be stuck."

Auryl didn't deny it, and that made up Kiara's mind for her. She sighed.

"Fine. A soul to catch, a love to find, moments of peril will soon unwind hearts too closed and thoughts too bound. I give my consent with arms unbound."

"Good job! You remembered!"

The tiny dragon sounded entirely too pleased. Kiara was tempted to call forth a bit of fire to singe Auryl's tail, but she reminded herself that condescending was the only tone most dragons knew how to use, *and* that just because this one was tiny didn't mean it couldn't destroy her with a single flex of its magic.

Now that Kiara had said the spell, she saw that the mirror on the wall in front of her was changing. The golden glow that had been lighting up the small room was now fading to just the edges and a clear portal was opening into... a very dense green forest. Kiara sighed and dismissed her playing card as she tugged the sleeves of her greatcoat into place. Then she stepped right up to the portal and began to stick her hand through. Like every portal she'd ever encountered, it parted around her skin like warm water and she could feel a faint breeze on the tips of her fingers as her wrist began to push through. Only when she'd already put one foot through the portal and was physically committed to heading to the other side lest she risk tearing herself in half did she hear Auryl's voice cheep after her in such a rush that it all sounded like one incredibly drawn out word: "safetyandsurvivalnotguaran-

teedtrueloveonlyexperiencedifbothpartiesfindeachother
acceptablesteppingthroughtheportalconstituesacceptan-
ceofthesetermspleasedon'tbeangryKiaraIpromiseyou'll-
beokifyouworktogether"

"Son of a—" But before she could even finish her sentence Kiara found herself stumbling out of the portal and into one of the darkest and most obviously cursed forests she'd ever seen.

LYRA HEARD THE curse from the ground behind her and felt torn between relief and trepidation.

A very loud part of her brain was damned glad to have someone else in here with her. The last half an hour had been as unsettling as it was strange. She'd reluctantly agreed to Auryl's childish sounding spell contract and then been horrified by the burst of verbal small print that the tiny dragon had uttered right as she stepped through the portal. Then she'd promptly forgotten what the tiny dragon had said because she'd been too distracted by her surroundings. The first thing she'd noticed had been the smell, which was actually a fairly normal forest smell: damp earth, green leaves, and the faint scent of rot that accompanied thick undergrowth. What had surprised her had been how dark the forest on this side of the portal was—darker than the height and expanse of the canopy above her really warranted. She'd first explored the immediate surroundings on foot, and had been disturbed to find that the only obvious foot path was blocked by a magical barrier. The portal had deposited her at the top of a small rise, but the trees around her were too tall and too dense to allow for any kind of a view. When she'd tried to follow the small footpath that led away from the portal, she'd bounced off an invisible barrier that felt like a stage curtain pulled tight, and when she'd tried to wander off through the trees instead, she'd encountered the same barrier. Eventually, after bouncing off the barrier in every direction she could think of, she'd given up and decided to get some perspective.

The first tree she tried to climb had literally shaken her off, and she'd simply glared at it for a moment before trying another one. When that one had done the same thing, she gave up on the trees and started to inspect the thick green vines dangling down from some of the higher branches. The vines had gotten very interested in her when she'd first started to climb them, attempting to curl around her ankles and occasionally her wrists. She'd managed to slap them off her wrists and keep moving her legs fast enough that they couldn't ensnare her as she climbed, but now that she'd been up here inspecting the view for a few minutes, she was going to need to disentangle her legs from the vines before she could start her descent.

The view hadn't told her much, unfortunately, but now that someone else was here maybe she could make use of what little she had learned. She hoped the person who had arrived was actually someone she could trust. She couldn't help but mistrust Auryl's motives now that she was here and could see that this forest was clearly cursed. What kind of matchmaker sent their clients into cursed forests on a first date?

Since none of the answers that came to mind for that question were reassuring, she figured whoever had just stumbled through that portal could just as easily be here to kill her as help her.

Then, of course, there were the first date jitters that she was inexplicably still riddled with, despite the fact that this whole thing was seeming less and less like a real date and more and more like an easy way to die young.

She swallowed hard and took another look at the narrow path that strung off into the distance; as long as that barricade dropped now that her "date" was here, that trail should be their ticket out of here. Lyra shuddered, though. This forest was absolutely slathered in malicious magic, which she could feel from here even though it seemed to largely be restrained by the barricade that had kept her off of the path.

Having acquired as much information as she could reasonably gather from her climb into the canopy, she set up a simple leg wrap that would get her all the way to the forest floor without any help from her arms. Then, while she descended, she did her best to make sure that her top and hair were in some kind of order.

She hadn't had the time or energy to go home and change between closing up the café and going on this date, so she'd been forced to put on some of her performance gear from the aerial bag she kept stuffed under the counter. She didn't mind wearing the tight but stretchy leggings she usually donned for performances, but the top was a bit lower cut and more form fitting than she might have chosen for a first date. Not that she minded showing off her cleavage, but, well—she generally preferred to draw her partners in with her personality before she put her breasts on quite this level of display.

The only other option had been her café tunic, which was covered in coffee stains, flour, and mystery food smears, so… she'd decided to err on the side of cleavage. Straightening out her performance top was quick work, and pulling the leaves from her hair was the best she could really manage before her thigh wrap had brought her to the forest floor. When she was a few feet off the ground, she grabbed the vine above her, swung her legs clear (a normally graceful move that was made far less elegant by the vine doing its best to grab onto her leg again), then dropped to the moss-covered earth and looked up.

Her breath caught.

The woman who stood before the portal had dark-grey skin, short silver hair that was casually messy in the way that a lot of people paid good money for, and delicately pointed ears. She was tall with an athletic build, not as slight as most half-elves. The purple tunic and black leather pants that were visible through the gaps in her coat suggested exactly the kind of body that Lyra appreciated in a woman. Lyra had about three heartbeats to appreciate how well Auryl's magic must work if it had found someone who was this much to her preferences in the span of a few hours—before her brain processed the meaning of the rest of the woman's attire. The heavy leather greatcoat, tall leather boots (although surprisingly high heeled), and crackling fire that surrounded the playing card flipping from one knuckle to the next all combined to smother the attraction and hope that had briefly flared inside her.

"Battle mage?"

Her throat had worked without her even meaning it to, and she hated how disappointed her voice sounded to her own ears. But the flood of memories that rushed back to her, along with the crushing weight of remembered loss, was more than she could swallow. She tried to shake it off her body as if it were nothing more than overtaxed muscles, but that did little to revive the attraction she'd first felt. And, when she looked up at the beautiful woman with the enthralling purple eyes a second time, she managed only a weak smile.

K IARA WAS ON fire. Or she thought she was on fire. Had she let her magic slip and lit up her entire body by accident? There was a goddess descending from a tree as if the vines themselves were slowly delivering her to the ground. Had Kiara ever seen a woman that beautiful before? She was short and curvy, but amid the curves Kiara could see muscles rippling as she held herself in place on a vine as thick as Kiara's forearm with nothing more than her thighs. Was it strange that Kiara was jealous of a vine? That was probably an inappropriate thought to have. The woman had purple skin and dark emerald hair that hung down to her waist. She was wearing leggings that showed off every one of the many muscles in her legs and a fitted top that plunged low, showing off enough of her cleavage to make Kiara swallow hard.

Then the words, "Battle mage?" and the tone—as if it were a prison sentence she'd been hoping to avoid—sank in, and the fire coursing through her veins turned to ice.

Kiara took a moment to survey the scene while she tried to compose herself. The forest around them was dark, suffused with menacing magic, and alive in ways that were likely to be problematic if they stayed here long. She restrained a sigh and turned back to the petite goddess who wanted nothing to do with her.

"Battle Mage Kiara Mefysta at your service," Kiara announced, bowing to cover up the disappointment that she was sure must be clear on her face. If the way she had said "Battle Mage" was anything to go by, the gorgeous woman apparently thought as little of Kiara's chosen profession as Evain had.

Not fit for a normal life. The words echoed in her memory even as she stared at the moss beneath her boots. Apparently, wearing her greatcoat had been the right idea after all; she'd saved herself and her date from a few hours of meaningless conversation, at least. She cleared her throat, and was about to suggest that they head back through the portal to ask Auryl to give up this farce, when she heard the other woman curse.

Chapter Three
Charisma Check

"Fuck. That little dragon had better not be trying to kill us," Lyra said, as she watched the portal that she could see just over the battle mage's shoulder wink out with a brief flash of gold light.

"The—Oh, gods damn it!" The other woman had whipped around so fast her greatcoat had gotten momentarily snagged in the trees. "And not a trace for me to follow either."

Lyra tried not to be pleased that the battle mage seemed as flustered as she felt. She reminded herself that she didn't know this woman at all, and that judging anyone else based on her own experience with Rylan was probably completely unfair. Not to mention that enjoying someone else's discomfort would be petty, even if the woman *had* deserved it. But all the beautiful half-elf had done was come through the portal and introduced herself, so she definitely didn't deserve it. Yet.

Oh gods, Lyra had NOT realized how bitter she still felt about her last relationship.

She took a deep breath and let it out slowly.

Og's balls, she was going to have to be careful about this. She cleared her throat.

"There's a trail that leads—well, I was going to say east, but these woods are so cursed I have no idea if the sun is even presenting accurately, plus the fog is so thick it's hard to make out which direction the sun is coming from to begin with—but let's call it 'east' for now."

Oh great, and now she was babbling. *No one needs your monologued backstory, Lyra, just stick to the point.* She coughed to cover her embarrassment for a moment, but the battle mage didn't say anything in the silence so she pushed on.

"So, yeah, there's a trail that leads east. Also, there was a barrier I bounced off of earlier when I tried to scout ahead that stopped me from following the trail or heading through the woods, but I wouldn't be surprised if it's gone now. It felt like it was tied to the portal."

When the mage just stared at her blankly for almost a full minute, she added, "My name's Lyra, by the way. You said you're Kiara? Nice to meet you. I'm sorry if I came across as rude earlier. I um... I don't have the best history with battle mages."

She couldn't read much on the mage's face, but she had a feeling that Kiara had no idea what to make of her.

"Are you an adventurer too?" the grey-skinned half-elf asked. "I don't recognize you from any of the Guild meetings."

Lyra couldn't help but laugh at the idea.

"Me? No way. I'm way too soft for that. I'm a simple hearth witch. I run the café that hosts that little broom cupboard." Lyra wanted to hide her face in her hands.

Too soft? Simple hearth witch? Here she sat, parroting every bullshit thing Rylan had ever said to her. *Great. Way to stick up for yourself, Ly! Definitely going to get better results if you lead with all your exes' wrong-headed ideas about you, right?*

"Nothing simple about being a hearth witch," Kiara said, with a level of sincerity that brought a smile to Lyra's lips. "And what exactly constitutes too soft for the Adventurer's Guild? No one with thigh muscles that solid could possibly be considered too soft for adventuring."

Was Lyra imagining the flush in Kiara's cheeks when she said that? It was hard to tell with elves sometimes, but she could have sworn that the other woman's neck and cheeks had flushed a deeper shade of grey when she'd mentioned Lyra's thighs. *Hmm... Interesting. I'm not sure I mind that she noticed my thighs, actually.*

But Lyra flicked the thought away. It didn't matter if the battle mage found her to be the sexiest woman alive. Sure, not all battle mages were the same, but they all had the same job. And no battle mage was ever going to accept Lyra the way she was now. She swallowed down the small warmth that the other woman's gaze and comment had brought to her chest and decided to skip past Kiara's other questions.

"The trail head is this way," she said, turning and waving towards the small dirt path that was the only way through the dense forest as far as she could see.

"Alright, but—"

Whatever objection the mage had been about to level was swallowed up by an ear-splitting shriek from somewhere in the woods behind them.

Where the portal had been only moments before was now a forest just as dark, menacing, and probably cursed as the forest ahead of them, but the trail only led in one direction, and the shriek had been followed by a very loud crashing sound. One that suggested multiple trees being felled by… something very large and very angry.

"Yes, right. Trail. Excellent plan," Kiara agreed quickly, as she joined Lyra in striding towards the aforementioned trail.

This time, when Lyra stepped onto the trail with Kiara at her side, no barrier stopped her.

SOUNDS OF RUSTLING in the dense woods all around them followed in their wake. The forest was unnaturally dark, smelled of old magic and damp earth, and occasionally tried to grab them with roots and vines. And *yet*. Kiara found most of her focus was on trying *not* to watch the way Lyra walked. She couldn't help but notice all the ways the other woman's muscles coiled and uncoiled as she moved. But what took the most effort to avoid was the way the parts of her that *weren't* muscle bounced. Kiara was really trying, though. Truly, she was. This might have been a date, technically speaking, but even still she was not the type of woman to ogle someone who hadn't specifically requested to be ogled. The ear-splitting shrieks and sounds of rending wood coming from behind them *should* have helped. After all, they made it much harder to appreciate anything beyond basic survival instincts. But those terrifying sounds were also making Lyra *walk faster*, occasionally dipping into a jog.

Watching Lyra jog, or trying desperately and failing *not* to watch her jog, was really making it difficult for Kiara to remember the whole list of reasons she was unfit for romantic entanglement. In the pauses between mysterious shrieks and terrifying forest sounds, Kiara went over the litany in her mind:

1. I court death every time I go to work. That's no foundation for a loving family.

2. How can anyone be expected to love me when my work means I might never come home every time I leave the house?

3. Weren't 1 and 2 basically the same thing, though? Focus, Kiara. Focus. Right. Umm… Oh yes, how could I possibly want children who might have to grow up without me? That's utterly selfish.

Est could say whatever she liked about Evain "ruining her," but Kiara had known all of those things to be true long before her ex had used them as reasons to end things. Evain had only reminded Kiara that she wasn't worth the risks her partner or future family would have to endure, only to be with her between assignments.

If she'd needed any more evidence, the face the hearth witch had made the moment she'd recognized Kiara for a battle mage was more than enough. No one needed to be put through that, and Kiara was honestly just glad that Lyra had remembered for both of them before Kiara let physical attraction get the best of her.

Kiara had never been good at corralling her heart. That's why she'd stopped dating altogether after Evain. She knew she couldn't spend time getting to know another woman, learning all the things that made her lovable and unique, just to have to end things before they got serious. Kiara's heart leapt to serious with a few shared jokes and a handful of favorite books in common. She had no business going on dates at all if she wanted to keep her heart intact.

"For Est," she whispered to herself as she worked to keep her eyes on the curving trail instead of the curvy hearth witch.

"What was that?" asked Lyra.

"Nothing. Just remembering something."

"Oh, well, got any ideas about what in the hells is making that noise?" Lyra's voice was pretty level, but Kiara *thought* she could detect just the barest hint of anxiety in it—which was impressive, since Kiara herself was about ready to crap in her leggings the next time that gods-awful screech sounded.

"No idea. That is unlike any sound I've ever had the displeasure to hear," she replied.

"Oh." That seemed to throw the other woman off for a moment. "Well, that's not reassuring. Unless you're new to the whole adventurer thing?" Lyra's voice might have contained a hopeful edge, but Kiara shook her head and tried to keep her eyes on the trail.

"I'm afraid not. Eighteen years in."

"Eighteen years? Did you…"

Lyra's voice trailed off, even as she reached a hand to the lovely pendant at her neck, and though Kiara was *very* curious to hear whatever Lyra had been about to ask, a loud crashing sound to the left of them took all of her attention before she could follow up.

Kiara kept her eyes on the forest and her hands ready to call fire. She was vaguely aware of Lyra whispering something while clutching one hand to her chest, but she couldn't spare the attention to figure out what the other woman was doing, and before she could ask, a monster crashed through the forest and onto the path immediately behind them.

"WHAT THE FUCK is that?" Lyra squeaked in a much higher pitch than she intended.

She'd been trying to ignore the terror-inducing sounds of the cursed forest—not just the shrieks coming from behind them, but also odd echoing calls of animals that Lyra didn't recognize and didn't particularly want to meet. Meanwhile, the enveloping darkness from the trees that loomed overhead, branches and vines mingling into a low arch that was barely taller than Kiara, was harder to ignore. The thick mist that flowed through the trees and felt like clammy fingers reaching between the gaps in her clothes was unpleasant, to say the least, but the worst was the sensation of the various branches and roots that kept reaching for her and Kiara's ankles, consistently wrapping around her whenever she paused for even a single heartbeat, tugging as though they were trying to pull her into the dense woods just beyond the trail. Lyra would be too terrified to move if she let it have her attention, so she'd been trying to let it wash into the background of her perception by focusing on putting one foot in front of the other with a determination that she usually reserved for training sessions for the Night Guild. And it had almost worked.

She'd been a breath away from relaxing enough to ask if the battle mage had known her aunt, Violet. But then she'd realized at the last second that she would be broaching a topic sure to make herself cry, and while she generally had no reservations about crying in front of other people, the last thing she needed was for the battle mage to have even *more* reasons to think she was soft. Not to mention the noises she made when she really got going might attract even worse things than whatever was already following them.

She'd been so concerned with selecting a topic of distracting conversation that had nothing to do with her aunt that the strange creature crashing onto the trail behind them had almost been a relief. Almost. But the thing was so strange and startling that she'd reached for Aunt Vi's pendant and whispered a call to Gwen all the same.

The creature that had appeared on the trail looked like nothing so much as a writhing pile of vines. In that first moment, Lyra thought that she'd seen a glimpse of varnished brown and a glint of bronze somewhere in the green mass that was flailing across the ground like a wayward sea creature—but no sooner had she seen it than the vines shifted again and it was gone.

Lyra had never heard of a creature like this one, even in the wildest stories her aunt had spun, and the battle mage beside her didn't seem to have any explanation either.

"I honestly don't know," Kiara murmured. And it took Lyra three full heartbeats before she realized that Kiara was answering her question.

The reason they both had time to stop and ponder the thing for so long was that the creature didn't seem at all interested in attacking them. Its vines flapped wildly around it in a manner Lyra thought *could* be interpreted as threatening, but, if anything, the writhing mass of vines looked a bit stunned. As if breaking out of the dark forest mere moments ago was an unexpected turn of events. Of course, it wasn't as though the creature had a face, so Lyra wasn't entirely sure what gave her that impression, but she had it all the same.

But before Lyra or Kiara could begin to speculate on the creature's true intentions, not to mention what the thing might *be*, it released the same earsplitting shriek they'd been hearing for past few minutes, a sound that at this distance caused both Lyra and Kiara to drop to their knees and cover their ears. Then, moving with a speed that should have been impossible for a chaotic mass of wriggling vines, it charged towards them.

Lyra did her best to roll out of the thing's way but still found herself partially trampled by a half-dozen flailing green limbs. For a moment she lost all sense of direction as she tumbled through a writhing mass of green that surrounded her on all sides until she was left lying on her side at the edge of the packed dirt path as the… whatever-it-was shot past them onto the trail ahead.

She was relieved to see that Kiara was also lying on the trail, apparently unhurt, though clearly as confused as Lyra. But that relief lasted only a few seconds before a much louder crashing sound from behind them was quickly followed by an enormous tree trunk and a giant bugbear thrashing onto the trail.

"Well, at least now we know what it was running away from," Lyra whispered.

Kiara said nothing, but she'd already summoned fire to both of her hands.

Lyra's hands went immediately to Aunt Violet's pendant, but when they reached her neck, she found nothing there. She would have started panicking then—since that pendant was not only priceless but also her best defense against anything that wanted to hurt her—but she didn't have time to panic, as the enormous bugbear chose that moment to scream like the unquiet dead while turning straight towards them.

Chapter Four
Agility Check

"Run," Kiara told her, as she turned to face the bugbear.

Lyra did her best not to scoff at this. It wasn't that she thought she'd be particularly useful in a battle against something three times the height of her much taller date. It was just that running would be an exercise in futility. She knew nothing about where this trail went, except that there was a shrieking vine monster a little way ahead of them, and that the forest was liable to eat her if she slowed down for more than a single breath. Meanwhile, it wasn't as though standing alone just a bit farther down the trail was going to keep her safe from this bugbears' friends—and if Aunt Vi's stories had taught her anything, it was that bugbears normally traveled in groups.

Though she was already starting to get the feeling that this particular bugbear wasn't what one would call 'normal.' In that eerie time-slowing moment before the enormous creature screamed and charged at them, Lyra couldn't help but notice that the creature's skin was sagging in a way that did not seem entirely healthy, and that its eyes had the cloudy film over them that usually accompanied death. None of which was comforting.

Regardless, running would have been stupid.

But that didn't mean she should just stand here and get clobbered by any number of bugbears—no matter how abnormal they were—or the stray spells that Kiara was likely to start lobbing in her own defense.

"Gwen, please tell me you materialized before Vi's pendant went missing," Lyra breathed as she reached up for the nearest vine that was trying to wrap around her neck, shook it like a misbehaving dire-weasel, and then started to climb.

KIARA SLAPPED ANOTHER errant vine away from her shoulder, tried to block the sudden and intense smell of rotting flesh that now permeated their overly crowded stretch of dark, misty foot path, and ruminated on how very little she enjoyed fighting bugbears. Not that there was any group of people or creatures that she *did* enjoy fighting in particular. She really was quite content to leave most living souls alone, so long as they left her alone. Of course, her job made that a lot more complicated, as she and her team were often sent off for the express purpose of not leaving "monsters" alone. Despite this, she and her crew had a strict policy about clearing up any potential misunderstandings between the supposed monsters they were sent to confront and whoever had called on the Adventurer's Guild. They weren't in the habit of killing someone just because that someone had fur and fangs. Luckily, the Guild policies backed them up, so if anyone got funny ideas about who deserved killing, Kiara and her team didn't have to worry about the Guild reprimanding them for making sure no innocent non-humans got a beating.

Bugbears were no more likely to cause trouble than any other group of people, but they did have the unfortunate habit of being very large and very grumpy. So, a bugbear who had been falsely accused of creating trouble was 100% more likely to be causing trouble after the accusation, regardless of whether or not it was true. Furthermore, bugbears were big enough and strong enough that Kiara had no interest in tangling with them by herself. At least not up close. And this one was far too close.

It also looked weirdly unstable. In fact, it looked like it was falling apart—and not just metaphorically.

"Zombie bugbear," Kiara muttered, "Fuck my life." And then the time for talking was over.

Kiara rolled out of the way of the bugbear's first lunge and snapped a card to her fingertips as she rose from the ground. When she flicked the card, it formed a blue bubble that surrounded both her and Lyra an instant before the bugbear smashed into it at full speed.

"Ew," came Lyra's voice from somewhere above and behind her.

"Yeah, that's officially gross," Kiara agreed, without taking her eyes off the bugbear.

Kiara had only fought bugbears a handful of times before, but she was fairly certain that they weren't meant to leak green goop from… well, everywhere. She was even more certain that the bugbear's eyeballs were meant to stay in its head… which meant that this bugbear was having a particularly awful day. And yet, the creature didn't even seem phased by the various bits of itself that remained stuck to Kiara's shield when it pulled away in order to raise its giant club.

"You might want to stay back," Kiara said. "I'm going to have to drop my shield in order to toast this thing."

"You may not want to—" Lyra began, but Kiara didn't have time to listen to whatever the hearth witch planned to say because the bugbear was already swinging at Kiara's shield, and if she was going to roast the bugbear without setting either herself or Lyra ablaze, she had to time this perfectly.

The bugbear roared, either to hype itself up or call for backup; when it did, green spittle flew out of its mouth, and the sight of the horrid emerald slime was almost enough to stop Kiara from dropping her shield. She did *not* want to get that stuff on her, but if she let the bugbear get closer, then she would have no way to fry it without frying herself and Lyra, too. So she braced herself for the disgusting goop and dropped her shield, just as she flicked her ace to the other side and flung it, engulfing the bugbear in her favorite close-range fireball.

L YRA SHIFTED HER weight on the thick vine wrapped around her leg, adjusted her grip on the vine above her, did her best to ignore the stench rising from the trail far below, and then cursed under her breath.

Battle mages. Og's balls. She could see the confident smirk that had started to form on Kiara's face when she flicked her fireball at the zombified bugbear, but even as she watched, the mage's face fell from confidence to frustration.

"What the fuck?" Kiara asked the now flaming bugbear. Probably because it didn't have the decency to even cry out in pain, let alone collapse in a heap as the mage had probably expected, now that it was on fire.

"I think it's undead," Lyra called down from where she was swinging from her vine a good fifty feet above the trail they had been following.

"Yeah, but—" Kiara's reply came in fits and starts as she was now playing a very awkward but high stakes game of tag with the flaming bugbear. "Even… undead… things… burn."

"Well, it's burning, it just doesn't give a fuck," Lyra replied, trying to mask her annoyance.

"Yeah, but come on, how is that fair? Now I'm just fighting a flaming bugbear."

"I did try to warn you," Lyra replied just as she lined herself up with the bugbear beneath her. "Kiara, can you roll away from the flaming bugbear on three?" she asked.

"Sure, but what—"

Lyra didn't have time to discuss her plan if it was actually going to work. So she had to hope that Kiara wasn't going to get herself killed through sheer stubbornness.

"One, two, three!"

Luckily, for all that the battle mage probably thought Lyra was insane for giving her orders, she took them. Which is how Lyra was able to drop her great grandmother's steel sewing table straight onto the bugbear's head from fifty feet up.

[illegible]

Probably [illegible]

[illegible] different [illegible]

[illegible] photo [illegible]

[illegible]

[illegible]

Chapter Five
Wisdom Check

"Dag's tits! What in the hells was that?" Kiara shouted as the bugbear went from towering, flaming monster to lightly flaming stain on the trail in a single blink.

Lyra's voice came from somewhere in the mist-shrouded darkness above the trail. "That was Great Gram's original Slinger 300."

Kiara looked up just in time to see Lyra descending from a vine like a goddess, *again*, using nothing but a friction wrap and her thighs. Kiara was not getting used to that. She could already feel heat creeping into her neck and chest, so she took a deep breath, and was instantly distracted from any and all inappropriate thoughts as she nearly choked on the stench of burning zombie.

"Where in the name of Og's left testicle did you find a two-hundred-pound sewing machine in the middle of a cursed forest?" she asked, when she could finally get enough air to speak.

"It's a three-hundred-pound sewing machine, thank you very much, and I didn't find it. I had it with me."

Kiara couldn't help it; she looked over Lyra's outfit to see where she could possibly have stuffed the giant sewing machine that now lay atop the squished bugbear. The massive metal device was hardly any worse for wear, even after being dropped from halfway up an enormous cursed tree.

Lyra reached the ground a few moments later, and then headed over to the pile of sewing machine and former bugbear.

"Damn. Broke the pedal. Forthwright is going to be pissed at me when I bring it in to fix again. She told me not to bother her with anything that wasn't a weapon after the last time. Do you think she'd let it slide this once since it's *technically* a weapon now?"

Kiara couldn't stop the laugh that broke out of her then. Not just a small chuckle but a truly embarrassing belly laugh, followed swiftly by a cackle. She may even have snorted.

"I can't believe you just demolished an undead bugbear with a sewing machine. That has got to be, hands down, the most obscure kill I've ever heard of, and I have been adventuring for the better part of two decades."

Lyra's cheeks flushed a deeper shade of purple and Kiara tried very hard not to think about how pretty that made the already gorgeous hearth witch.

"Aunt Vi would have been proud, that's for sure," Lyra admitted.

The moment the words were out of the café owner's mouth Kiara saw her eyes dart away and start to fill with tears. Then Lyra started to reach for her own neck, but hastily dropped her hand.

"Who is Aunt Vi?" Kiara asked, doing her best to keep her voice gentle. It was obvious that whoever Aunt Vi was, talking about her was pretty emotional for Lyra.

Lyra shook her head for a moment, and Kiara didn't know if it was because she didn't want to talk about it or because she couldn't get her voice to work. So Kiara just waited and brought a new ace to her fingertips to keep herself from reaching out and brushing the tears away from Lyra's eyes.

"Aunt Vi was the woman who raised me," Lyra said, after a long pause and a few attempts to clear her throat. "She died a few years ago, and… I'm not over it yet."

Lyra gave a self-deprecating laugh as she said the last part, and Kiara took a deep breath in order to steady her voice before she spoke.

"Of course you're not," Kiara said, her voice still gentle, but firmer this time. "No one could expect you to be over it yet. Grief like that lasts a lifetime. You don't ever 'get over it,' you just learn not to poke the tender bits as hard most days."

Even saying the words brought too many memories to the surface and Kiara had to pause before she could speak again.

"I'm surprised someone who raised you would be particularly excited that you were fighting bugbears, though. Pretty risky business."

For some reason that made Lyra let out a full-throated laugh. Kiara enjoyed the sound of it almost as much as she enjoyed seeing a bit of light return to the other woman's eyes.

"Aunt Vi was a battle mage, like you," she explained. "She was in the Adventurer's Guild for about 50 years. She would be ecstatic that I was finally having an adventure of my own."

"Oh? What was Vi short for?"

Lyra smiled and had to clear her throat before she could speak. "Violet. If you knew her, you would have known her as Stranglevine, though. That was her Guild name."

"Mage Stranglevine was your mom?"

"Well, my aunt. But she raised me, yeah."

Kiara just blinked for a moment. Not even the smell of the singed undead bugbear decomposing a few paces away could shake her from all the questions that now jangled for attention in her brain. To her shame, the first one that popped out of her mouth was, "Mage Stranglevine raised a hearth witch?"

Kiara wanted to slap herself when she saw Lyra's smile fall away and the small spark of light leave her eyes.

"What? You can't imagine someone as grand and important as Mage Stranglevine raising someone as insignificant as a hearth witch?" Lyra asked, her voice oozing the bitterness of an oft-reopened wound.

"No, no!" Kiara objected. "Not like that. I just mean... she was always so... messy, and disheveled, and... gods, did you ever see her office at the Guild hall? I can't imagine a hearth witch living with her and not just setting all of her things on fire and then walking away."

The laugh that greeted that statement warmed Kiara all the way to her toes.

"I might have considered lighting some of her paperwork on fire a handful of times... but it's not like other people's messes really bother me. And it wasn't like she did it on purpose, she just..."

"Always thought she'd get to it later and then kinda never did?" Kiara asked.

"Yeah. Exactly that. How'd you know?"

"I *might* share that trait with your aunt," Kiara said, feeling her cheeks heat with the admission.

"Ah. Well, at this point, having a slovenly roommate just feels like home, so you'll get no judgment from me."

"You wouldn't say that if you saw my apartment," Kiara replied.

"You would understand why I don't judge, if you saw mine," Lyra teased.

"Well, if we survive all the way to the exit portal, I'll have to visit sometime."

Kiara felt her cheeks grow even warmer when Lyra didn't respond immediately, and she suddenly realized she'd just invited herself over to the woman's home!

"I mean, not if you don't want me to. That is, just to see the mess... or—shit. I didn't mean to invite myself over! Forget I said anything!"

Lyra laughed again, and that helped Kiara relax a bit.

"You are welcome to come see the mess some time, Mage Mefysta. Only, it's Kyle's mess and I'd probably tidy everything up if I knew we had a guest coming. My magic gets itchy when guests don't have room to sit on the couch."

"It does? Fascinating. I've always wondered about the compulsions in hearth magic. Is it the same as the compulsions in elemental magic, do you think? Like the way fire calls to me—is that how cleanliness calls to you?"

"I've heard that natural hearth mages feel that way, but I'm a trained hearth witch, so I wouldn't know."

"Ooh! Even more interesting! What's your natural element then?"

"Water," Lyra said, glancing at the trail and reaching her hand to her throat again. Kiara watched the motion with interest and then wondered if she was staring a little too pointedly at the hollow at the base of Lyra's throat and decided to look away.

"We should probably—" they both started at the same time.

Kiara nodded in deferral.

"Please, you first."

"We should probably get moving so that we're not just standing here when the next bugbear shows up, but I was wondering if we could keep an eye out for that... vine... monster... *thing* that we saw earlier? It took something from me. I think by accident, but, well, I can't leave without it."

"Of course! I'm so sorry. What did it take?"

Lyra took a deep breath and then sighed. "Aunt Vi's familiar."

T HEY'D ALREADY STARTED down the small dirt foot path again, mainly to get away from the smell of burnt zombie. Despite how all-encompassing the darkness of the woods felt, Lyra was able to watch Kiara's face go through the dawning realization of what she'd just said. Somehow, even with hardly enough moonlight to allow them to see the trail, Lyra was able to make out the slow rise of Kiara's silver eyebrows, the faint widening of her sclera, and the subtle opening of her mouth. She ignored how pretty the battle mage was and braced herself for the usual dismissive questions.

None of Vi's old colleagues had been able to believe that Vi had left Gwen to Lyra. They'd all assumed Vi would have left her familiar to the Guild, or perhaps to one of her former apprentices, but none of them had even considered that Lyra would want her. Even worse, they hadn't considered what *Gwen* had wanted for herself.

They'd only asked, *But how could you possibly handle a familiar like Gwen?* Or, *A hearth witch with a battle mage's familiar, how does that even work?* Or, *Oh, what a waste, that poor creature.* As if Lyra would let Gwen languish away just because she wasn't off fighting monsters every day. As if Gwen didn't want her company just as much as she wanted Gwen's.

But all Kiara said was, "We should move faster. I'm sorry I distracted us chatting. How long since you noticed the pendant was missing?"

Lyra swallowed down a stab of emotion that gutted her out of nowhere. Dag's tits, it wasn't like the woman had offered her hand in marriage or something, all she'd done was taken for granted that Gwen was where she was supposed to be.

Get it together, Ly.

"Not long after that vine thing crashed into us. It was there the last time I reached for it, before that thing crashed into the trail, and gone when I reached for it after. I summoned her before that, though. The shrieking scared me enough that I asked her to come. Then I asked Gwen if she could help us with the bugbear, but she had her own problems to deal with, and she didn't want to lose track of the vine creature."

"Oh. That makes sense. Well, I'm glad you'd already summoned her; that should make this a lot easier."

"It should, although cursed forests being what they are, I have a sneaking suspicion it still won't be *easy*."

"Fair point. Well made." Kiara nodded with each sentence.

"Ha! Vi used to say that all the time."

"That *may* be where I picked it up."

"Oh gods, you knew her that well? I should have known!"

Lyra watched Kiara's face and realized that the half-elf was blushing, at least in as much as pewter-grey elf skin could blush.

Kiara cleared her throat before saying, "I mean, she was my idol when I first got to the Guild. And she was my mentor for a little while there. Or, well… you know how few battle mages there are that live past their first ten years? I honestly think she kept us all at arm's length in those first few years because she didn't want to have to mourn the 25% of us who died stupidly before we learned that not all of our problems could be blasted away with sheer force."

Lyra felt her own mouth curving into a fierce smile.

"She used to talk so much shit about young battle mages, you wouldn't believe it," Lyra admitted. "She was never mean about anything people couldn't control, but she was absolutely ruthless about bad decisions by full-grown adults. Especially adults who signed up to be adventurers but whom she fully expected to die the first time they met a real threat."

Kiara chuckled. "I can imagine. And she had reason enough to think us dumb. A lot of us never made it past those early years."

Kiara swallowed, and Lyra immediately recognized the pain in the other woman's eyes.

"You lost friends?" Lyra asked, even though she already knew the answer.

Kiara nodded, probably unable to trust her voice in that moment. "Yeah," she eventually said. "It was almost twenty years ago now, but I'm still not 'over it.'"

Lyra heard the echo of her own words from earlier. She couldn't help but notice how Kiara's words weren't tinged with bitterness or self-recrimination, though. Just a statement of fact. Nearly twenty years and she still wasn't over it, but that was fine. That was just how it was. Grief took time. Sometimes, often, a lifetime. And Kiara wasn't going to hold that against herself or, apparently, anyone else.

Something small lightened in Lyra's chest with that thought.

Lyra didn't realize she was staring at the battle mage until Kiara cleared her throat again.

"I think it went this way." The battle mage gestured towards the side of the trail, and when Lyra's eyes followed the gesture, she didn't have to ask what made Kiara think that. Even Lyra's virtually non-existent tracking skills were sufficient to tell that something very large and not particularly coordinated had careened off the trail here and heedlessly plowed through whatever was in its way as it did so. There was a trail of snapped brush and ripped vines that was actually wider than the dirt path that they'd been following. It looked like a small hurricane had gone through the forest ahead of them.

"Wow. For a creature that was hell bent on running away from something, it sure leaves quite the trail."

"My guess is that stealth is not its strong suit."

"I dunno, it probably blends in to this place pretty well, with all those vines for legs."

"I'm not 100% convinced it's meant to have legs," Kiara mused.

"Do you know what it is then?"

"Nope. Not a clue. But… well, I mean, we just took out an undead bugbear, and this is *clearly* a cursed forest. Call it a hunch, but…"

"You think the vine creature was *cursed* to be the way it is now?"

"I wouldn't bet against it, is all I'm saying."

Lyra was letting Kiara lead the way since the battle mage insisted on periodically throwing flames at the little bits of forest that kept rising up trying to eat them. She had noticed, even as they'd started walking away from the squished and lightly flaming bugbear zombie, that the forest had been slowly wrapping the corpse in vines and dragging the pieces of it, even the still flaming ones, into the impenetrable dark of the underbrush. Since they'd already been walking *away* from the zombie bugbear's final resting place, Lyra hadn't even mentioned it, and only made a point of walking a bit faster. But now that they were off the trail, heading deeper into the forest, following the swath cut by the vine creature and listening to its intermittent shrieking, she was more than a little glad that the fire mage seemed all too willing to zap the various vines, roots, and even some rather aggressive fern leaves, that kept trying to grab them.

As she followed Kiara, who muttered a continual string of profanity while aiming very small bursts of fire at every handsy plant that came their way, Lyra did her best not to get nostalgic about trudging through the woods with a different battle mage, who was also gruff and swore a lot, but who was ultimately one of the kindest and most understanding people she'd ever known.

Aunt Vi would have loved this little excursion, carnivorous plants and all, and Lyra couldn't help but think that Vi would have loved Kiara too, but… *hmm…* well, it was possible she *had* loved Kiara or had at least liked her. Kiara had said Vi had been her mentor for a little while.

"So, did you and Aunt Vi actually get along once you survived your trial period?" Lyra asked at the next pause in Kiara's litany of swearing. She almost hated to bring it up again, because she knew how painful the topic might be for Kiara, not to mention for herself. But once she'd had the thought that Vi might have actually *known* the woman trudging through the forest zapping vines ahead of her, she suddenly couldn't let it go.

"Well, I'd say she tolerated me more than anything. She had her own friends from her own ranks in the Guild. We saw each other between assignments, and enjoyed swapping tales a few times, but you know… I always wondered where she was hurrying off to between jobs. She'd say she had to get back to her family, but when I asked around, folks said she didn't have a spouse or kids but… well, they were clearly wrong about the kid thing. She had *you*."

Lyra's throat tightened as more than one memory flooded into her, a series of relived moments in which Aunt Vi had come straight to Lyra when she'd gotten home from her latest assignment. Even though Lyra had been full grown—and completely able to take care of herself—by the time Vi went back to adventuring, Vi had invariably come to see her immediately when she returned home. She had always looked so exhausted, sometimes a bit battered or singed, but she'd always just looked so damned happy to see Lyra that… well, it almost made it easier to let Vi go again when her next assignment came along. Almost.

"Of course, I wasn't a kid anymore by the time you met Vi," Lyra added, once she was sure her voice wouldn't break on the words.

"Oh, I don't know about that. I started in the Guild pretty young."

"Well, regardless of how young *you* were, Vi didn't go back to the Guild until I was already apprenticed. Hence, not a kid. But how young could you have been? Didn't you train at the Mage Academy first?"

Kiara looked over her shoulder briefly after zapping another vine that was getting far too familiar with her ankle.

"I did, but umm… I graduated early."

"How early?"

"I finished at the Academy at eighteen."

"Isn't that the age a lot of folks START at the Academy?"

"It is. But… well, I started there at fifteen."

Lyra whistled low, and then a realization hit her.

"Wait, YOU'RE the child prodigy Vi used to go on about? The 'kid who could really make something of herself if she doesn't get killed in her first year?'"

Kiara whipped around and stared at Lyra, her hand poised to throw a fireball, and Lyra took a tiny step back, until a vine started slithering up her leg; she kicked it off and stepped closer to the fire mage again.

"Did your *aunt* say that to you?" Kiara asked, even as Lyra suddenly found herself standing close enough to the fire mage that she could smell leather, saddle soap, and a hint of wood smoke. She took a deep breath and then tilted her head up to look into the half-elf's deep purple eyes.

"Well, I think it was one of her colleagues who said the first part, but she used to say the second part often enough."

In an effort to distract herself from the heat that was climbing her neck as she looked into Kiara's eyes, Lyra thought for a moment about what all her aunt had said, and then she cackled.

"What?" Kiara asked, her purple eyes wide. She was still standing facing Lyra instead of the trail ahead of them, and Lyra was still standing far too close—but the laughter, and the memories, helped to distract her.

"I just put together that Vi was talking *you* up to me. She wanted to set us up on a date! She swore up and down that since you'd survived your first five years at the Guild, you clearly had a sensible head on your shoulders and…" Lyra's cheeks heated as she trailed off, unwilling to repeat the other thing Vi had said, desperately wanting to take a step back now that she'd thought of it, but also horribly aware of the plants behind her that were probably already reaching for her again.

"And what?" Kiara asked, her voice dropping and her gaze intense.

Oh gods, could Kiara possibly know what Vi had said and how it was making Lyra feel? No. That was ridiculous. *Keep calm, Ly. She can't read minds.*

"Nothing." Lyra could feel her cheeks, neck and chest flushing anyway.

Yes. Very smooth. She'll definitely believe that.

"No! What!? You can't just leave it there!" Kiara's voice was teasing, but she hadn't stepped away, and Lyra had no idea why they weren't currently getting swallowed by carnivorous ferns or something. It felt like they'd been standing in the same spot for minutes now.

"It's embarrassing," she finally admitted.

"For whom?" Kiara asked, her voice gentle.

"Umm... all involved?" Lyra's brain highlighted the precise words that Vi had used to describe Kiara to her once. Of course, Lyra hadn't known it was Kiara then, and Vi had never actually told her the name of the "prodigy mage" that she talked about occasionally and had tried to set her up on a date with only once.

"Come on, it can't be that bad," Kiara chided, still standing close enough that they were almost touching.

"Oh, it can, though," Lyra mumbled.

"My dear departed mentor was trying to set us up on a date, said nice things about me, and you refuse to tell me? Come on, that's cruel." Kiara's voice was both melodramatic and teasing, but Lyra thought that she was at least partially sincere.

Lyra sighed. She knew that Aunt Vi would have had no compunctions about telling Kiara what she'd said. It was just… well, it was a very forward thing to say, even repeated years later.

But Vi would have gleefully made fun of Lyra for being too shy to repeat the words, and that was ultimately what made her cave.

"She said… and remember it's been at least a decade since she brought it up last, so I may be misremembering the exact words but it was more or less… 'She's a tall drink of water and smart enough to keep you entertained. If I was twenty years younger, I wouldn't bother encouraging you, I'd just seduce her myself.'"

Lyra cleared her throat and looked away as she finished the quote. The darkness of the forest was intensely interesting, wasn't it? How many distinct species of plants had already tried to kill them, she wondered. Then she glanced back at Kiara.

Kiara blinked a few times.

"I thought your aunt preferred men?"

Lyra chuckled. "Apparently not exclusively."

"Fair enough."

There was another long pause during which Lyra had to look away from the grey-skinned, purple-eyed, white-haired half-elf and instead inspect the various types of vines that were still waving threateningly nearby.

Kiara swatted away a vine that was reaching for her neck, shot a tiny flame in its direction without turning around, and then asked, "So... why'd you say no?"

"I didn't, actually. I just hesitated for a while, and then Vi never mentioned it again; maybe because I started seeing someone not long after that, but I'm not sure. She had never mentioned you by name to begin with, so I had no inkling of who you were when you stumbled through the portal but..."

"But what?" Kiara seemed even closer than she had a moment before; Lyra wondered if that was true or just a trick of her mind.

"But I'm glad," Lyra said, her voice feeling far too breathy.

"You're glad?" Kiara asked, her purple eyes seeming to take up all of Lyra's vision.

"Glad that whatever strange magic Auryl uses to pair people up chose someone that Aunt Vi had met. Someone she liked. I know it doesn't mean anything, really. It's not like I would be seeking her approval for my partners if she were still alive, but… it's nice to meet someone for whom she isn't just a name and some old stories. She was real to you, too."

Kiara smiled, and it felt like the darkness of the woods was beaten back a tiny bit.

"Very real. Maybe too real."

Lyra and Kiara both laughed, the sound washing through the air like magic. Lyra's heart beat too loud in her chest, and she was just thinking that this would be the perfect moment to lean in and kiss the battle mage who looked so stupidly radiant when she laughed, but she hesitated for just a heartbeat…

And then another ear-splitting shriek rent the forest air behind them.

Suddenly, the forest seemed to remember their existence, and all at once, a dozen vines were grabbing for them both. Lyra fired off a few of her own weed-stopper spells to prevent the roots and vines that had gone for their ankles from succeeding, while Kiara zapped everything with more fire, and then they were off and running, doing their best to stay ahead of the plants that swarmed around them.

THIS WAS BAD. Not the plants, which for some reason had redoubled their efforts to kill them, or the desperate shrieking of the vine creature in the distance. Not even the running pell mell through half-broken underbrush without being able to see particularly well where they were going. Those things weren't *good*, but they were exactly what one expected in a cursed forest and Kiara knew how to handle them.

What was *bad* was that she had been so very close to asking if she could kiss the purple-skinned café owner. So close, in fact, that she'd almost been *relieved* when the shriek from somewhere ahead of them had ruined the moment. Somehow, Kiara had lost focus on her litany of reasons not to burden anyone else with her affections. Probably because her focus had been drawn to the shy grin on Lyra's face, and to how close they'd been standing, not to mention how the woman smelled like coffee and a hint of lemon. Worst of all, her focus had somehow drifted to thinking about how much more she wanted to hear about Lyra's life and her relationship with her aunt. Even though Kiara knew that the whole thing could only lead to disaster and she didn't need to put either of them through that. But damn it all, Lyra was just so… compelling? Curvy? Strong? Witty? And she must be one hell of a hearth mage if she could keep a familiar like Gwen happy and healthy.

Gwen. *Right. Yes. Good. Think about Gwen.* Concern for Gwen was the main reason she had started running after they'd heard that eerie shriek—well, concern for Gwen and also the fact that it seemed like all the plants had decided to attack at once after she and Lyra had stood in a single place gazing intently at each other for too long. *Gwen, Kiara, remember the nine-hundred-pound panther,* not *the intent gazing.* It had been ages since Kiara had seen Gwen, but she would never forget her. Half of the reason Kiara had idolized Mage Stranglevine had been because of Gwen. After all, even the most accomplished battle mages rarely had the ability to get a nine-hundred-pound panther from the ethereal plane on their side, but Stranglevine had never even struggled with it, and Gwen had never once tried to give her the slip.

Kiara had never adopted a familiar herself. Despite the number of times she'd projected to the ethereal plane, she'd never run into any creatures there that called to her soul the way she'd heard a familiar should, and the last thing she wanted was some poor ethereal tied to her existence for eternity without really wanting to be there. She still thought maybe someday she'd come across the right creature. After all, some mages found their familiars *much* later in life, and as a half-elf she had a quite a while to go before she reached anything close to what would be considered "old age," but she'd been adventuring for almost twenty years already and she hadn't found one yet. She wasn't exactly jealous of Lyra's familiar, but she did envy anyone who could have a close relationship with a soul like Gwen's.

Ah well, one more addition to the List of Things Kiara Can't Have Because of Who She Is and the Choices She's Made.

But if Gwen was in trouble, Kiara had no intention of letting her fight through it without help. Even as she crashed through the semi-cleared underbrush left by the fleeing vine creature, the surrounding woods so unnaturally dark that she could hardly see more than a few feet ahead at any moment, she pulled an ace from her sleeve, ready to cast a fireball or a shield at a moment's notice.

She should have known that it wasn't the nine-hundred-pound ethereal panther that was in trouble.

As she broke through the leaves and branches that separated her from a small clearing, she saw that the vine creature was the only one in trouble. Most of its vines were whipping wildly through the air, trying to keep a nine-hundred-pound purple panther at bay, which, of course, was only working because Gwen seemed surprisingly committed to *not* tearing the creature to bits.

Kiara took a brief moment to laugh at herself for ever having been worried about the panther in this scenario. Of course, she'd half-expected that the vine creature was somehow in cahoots with the zombified bugbears; not because that made any sense, but simply because it would be the most inconvenient way for things to go at this point—and honestly, that was just how Kiara's life went most days. But she should have remembered that the vine creature had obviously been running away from the bugbear, and it was unlikely that it had been running away because they were friends.

In the heartbeat before Kiara could decide how best to proceed, Lyra crashed into her back and took them both to the ground.

"Fuck," Lyra muttered, sounding completely terrified. "Sorry. Run!"

"What?" Kiara was distracted by the decidedly chaotic mixture of suddenly finding herself on the ground, an unknown number of vines reaching for various appendages, and the exceedingly pleasant sensation of having Lyra plastered so close to her that she could feel the woman's curves even through her leather greatcoat. It didn't help that Lyra's hair was falling all around them and her breasts were pushed firmly against Kiara's ribs.

"RUN!" Lyra shouted in Kiara's face.

Kiara was opening her mouth to explain how running was not going to happen, largely due to having her legs all tangled up with Lyra's, not to mention the vines. Also, she planned to explain that she'd just found Gwen, and the creature they'd been chasing, and shouldn't they do something about that before they ran off again? But then her gaze caught on the space where Lyra had just crashed through the brush, which was now occupied by three bugbears shuffling towards them at a much faster pace than she would have thought possible for zombies.

"Well, fuck," she had time to mutter, just before the shuffling bugbears reached the clearing.

YRA SMELLED SMOKE, felt the unmistakable heat of a fireball flying over her left shoulder, and decided that maybe running would have to wait. She did NOT want to find out what happened when she got closer to a fireball than she just had.

But given the way her legs were tangled with Kiara's, not to mention how the battle mage was now leaned up against her and lobbing flames over her shoulder, she couldn't get any farther away from the large balls of flame. So, she plastered herself even tighter against Kiara's side in an effort to give the woman more casting room, and meanwhile tried her best not to enjoy the feel of the other woman's lanky muscles pressed against her. She tried even harder to ignore the jolt of heat that surged through her when the mage wrapped one of her arms around Lyra in response.

She wasn't sure if Kiara had embraced her in order to keep her out of the line of fire, or just to give herself more room to maneuver, but Lyra's body decided all on its own that the sensation was worth melting over.

Gods, she was far too old to be feeling *that* kind of heat while dodging fireballs. What was wrong with her? The mage was busy trying to keep them from getting flattened by zombified bugbears for Dag's sake; she didn't need Lyra getting riled up like a teen witch who'd never touched another woman before.

Lyra felt something cold and slimy hit the back of her neck—which certainly did the job of dialing down her hormones—and she just barely stifled a scream. She really didn't want to know what had just dripped horribly down her neck, but she'd heard Gwen growling close by a moment ago, and she suspected that it might have been bugbear entrails.

Did you just disembowel a bugbear zombie all over my neck? she asked her aunt's familiar. Gwen didn't reply, but that didn't mean much. The panther didn't always enjoy chatting in the middle of a fight. With a jolt Kiara remembered she didn't have Gwen's charm anymore—not that she needed the charm to talk to the enormous panther when she was close by, but if she didn't get it back Gwen could wind up banished to the ethereal plane and Lyra would have no way to contact her there.

That was, after all, the whole reason they'd been running after the strange vine creature to begin with.

Og's balls.

Lyra looked up, a move she could just manage without getting all her hair singed off, as Kiara threw yet another fireball at the bugbears—why in Dag's name Kiara was still lobbing fireballs at them after how ineffective it had been last time, Lyra had no idea—and saw the vine creature slowly slinking off into the darkened forest while the bugbears, Gwen, and Kiara were all distracted trying to kill each other.

"Oh, hells no, you don't," Lyra muttered.

She waited just a heartbeat, because she could sense that Kiara was mid-cast and didn't want to interrupt her. But once the battle mage flicked her wrist and launched her latest attack at the bugbears, Lyra rolled out of the other woman's arms, pushed to her feet, and sprinted after the retreating vine creature. As she went, she sent up a quick prayer to all the gods that whatever the bugbears meant to do, they weren't close enough or aware enough to cut her down before she got out of the clearing.

"Be right back!" she yelled, not even looking behind her as she ran.

She had to hope that Gwen and Kiara had the bugbears in hand. She knew there was little she could do to help in close combat without taking the time to climb a tree—something that was a lot less likely to go unnoticed with three bugbears than a lone distracted one. She'd been lucky that circumstances had allowed her to drop a sewing machine on the first bugbear, and the chances that she'd be able to do that a second time were slim enough that she didn't feel particularly guilty running after the vine creature.

After all, if she could catch the vine creature and get Gwen's medallion back while Gwen and Kiara fought the bugbears, then she'd be out of their way AND doing something useful at the same time. As pleasant as it had been to lie pressed up against Kiara's lithe form while the fire mage lobbed spells over her head, Lyra really hated feeling useless. So she ran into the darkened woods just a few paces behind the writhing mass of vines that still had Gwen's pendant and hoped for the best.

Chapter Six
Disengage

KIARA REMINDED HERSELF that it was perfectly reasonable for a civilian to run away from three enormous zombie bugbears, and that, in fact, she would have an easier time fighting the damned things with just her and Gwen to worry about, rather than having Lyra in the mix. Her brain knew that was true, her good sense screamed at her that it was not only reasonable but also the correct choice for any sane person to make. But the part of her that had been wildly aware of every inch of Lyra's curves pressed against her was irrationally disappointed by their sudden departure.

And that part is just going to have to shut up and cope, damn it, she thought ruthlessly, as she stood up from the forest floor where she'd been pinned underneath Lyra until only a few moments ago.

The forest floor writhed with vines and roots, but for some reason they weren't trying to wrap her legs and ankles at the moment, so she refocused her efforts on the bugbears. It occurred to her that she really shouldn't have opened with fireballs, given she was now, yet again, fighting the damned zombies in close quarters—and that, yet again, they seemed completely unfazed by their fur, skin, and flesh being engulfed in flames.

Gwen, whose attacks were entirely tooth and claw based, was in even closer quarters with the flaming zombies, but luckily didn't seem to be at all affected by fire. That made sense, given that most ethereals were immune to elemental attacks.

Which gave Kiara an idea, now that Lyra was safely out of the clearing.

Kiara flicked two playing cards into her hands and shouted a quick warning to Gwen. Then she released two enormous fireballs straight at the three bugbear zombies.

YRA WAS PANTING like she'd just run a hundred league race when she finally caught up with the vine monster. It wasn't that the thing moved quickly—while it moved far more quickly than it had any right to, it was still too unwieldy to be faster than Lyra at a dead sprint. Plus, it kept getting hung up on bits of forest and underbrush as it went. But while the vine creature didn't seem to care what stood in its path and blithely plowed straight ahead, Lyra had found that without Kiara at the front burning everything in their way, there were now dozens of plants, logs, rocks, small streams, and possibly even a few living creatures (though it was hard to tell given how quickly she passed them) that she needed to climb over, jump across, swing around (while clinging to whatever vines she could reach), and otherwise dodge away from, that really made this pursuit a full-body workout.

Maybe she'd mention this to their choreographer at the next training session for the Night Guild. Perhaps a cursed forest obstacle course was just what their troupe needed to get them through the next round of rehearsals and their upcoming show? Or maybe she was just having too much fun chasing after a weird vine creature in the woods and she really needed to calm down before she got killed thanks to a random adrenaline high.

Oh gods, this was what Vi had always warned her about, wasn't it? Vi had often said that adventuring was like a drug. Once you got over the sheer terror of it, the joy of survival and the challenge of solving problems all added up to something you couldn't say no to.

Lyra winced. She'd never been particularly drawn to the idea of constantly wandering the world looking for trouble, despite Vi's glorified tales of heroics. It had all sounded thrilling, of course, but... it had never sounded particularly *satisfying* to Lyra. Now she wondered if she'd been wrong about that, or if she was just riding a high that would let her crash as soon as she was on the other side of danger.

She shook the thought away for the time being and focused on the task ahead of her.

Namely the vine monster, which was not only ahead of her, but which seemed to be finally holding still. Which was a relief right up until Lyra noticed that it was holding eerily still in a clearing filled with a strange light. The light was disconcerting, since the forest around them was as unnaturally dark as it had always been—even when she'd climbed her way up to the canopy earlier, the sky had been too full of mist and clouds to allow much light through. But most disconcerting of all was the strange whining keen that seemed to be coming from the vine creature.

Lyra stopped short of the clearing and thought for a moment.

Vi had been very clear on one rule as she raised Lyra—even though Lyra had never planned to become an adventurer—*Never walk into a situation you don't understand.* Lyra had no idea what was going on with the vine creature or the clearing filled with strange light, and she didn't think walking into the clearing was a safe way to find out. So she fell back on her old standby: get some perspective.

Apparently, she'd been standing still for too long, because a vine reached down and slithered over her shoulder towards her neck. Instead of swatting it away as she normally would have, she grabbed the end of it and gave it a hard pull. When it stayed securely attached to whatever part of the canopy it had come from, she grabbed it with her left hand as well and tested it with her full weight.

She'd left the bugbears, Kiara, and Gwen long behind by now, but she still checked over her shoulder briefly to make sure she wasn't about to get clubbed to death before her next move.

Then she tipped her head back and launched her legs upward, wrapping her right leg around the vine so that she could grab it with the back of her knee. From there, she used the friction provided by her right knee along with the counterweight of her left leg to lever herself upwards so that she could grab the vine above and switch to an upright climb.

"Who'd have thought that a cursed forest would be such good aerial practice?" she muttered to no one.

In short order, she was fifty feet above the ground and absolutely horrified at the sight revealed below her.

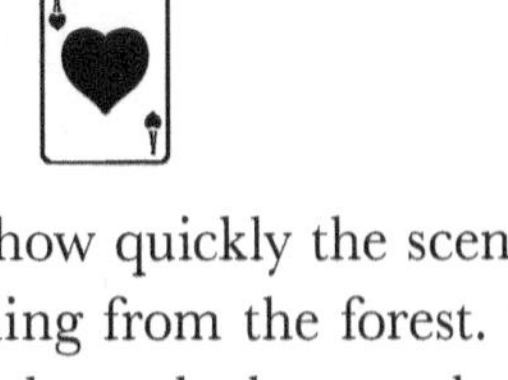

KIARA WAS SURPRISED at how quickly the scent of burning bugbear was fading from the forest. She glanced around the densely packed trees, dangling vines, and enormous broad-leafed plants that surrounded her, and failed to repress a shiver when confronted with how quickly and efficiently the vines, roots, and earth of the forest had grabbed, and reclaimed, the zombie-infernos she'd created with her storm of fireballs.

The plan had been to take advantage of her own imperviousness to fire (and Gwen's) in order to burn the bugbears to ash. Zombies weren't stopped by fire, mostly because they didn't feel pain, not because it didn't actually burn them. If you cast *enough* fire at them, they would eventually stop moving—if only because piles of ash didn't move particularly well.

But the plan hadn't worked.

Or, well… the plan had worked differently than she'd expected.

Once the bugbears were burning so brightly that everything they touched seemed to catch fire, the cursed forest had apparently decided to intervene.

Kiara was still reeling from just how quickly the cursed forest's vines, roots, leaves, and dirt had all rushed as one to envelop the zombie infernos and… well… extinguish them. It had pulled them in every direction at once, only to bury the pieces inside of trees, pits of earth, and wherever else the forest could put out the flames. She hadn't exactly been able to keep track.

The sound of rending flesh and bone still echoed in Kiara's ears.

Now, Kiara was wiping bugbear guts off of her boots and wishing they'd been spelled as thoroughly as her greatcoat, which had shed the mess the forest had created with ease.

"Bugbear guts and leather don't mix, Gwen," she muttered.

I could have told you that, but the forest didn't seem to care about your clothes when it ripped that last one apart.

Kiara's eyes snapped to the giant panther's. That voice had sounded in her mind like a thought that wasn't her own. Gwen's enormous, glowing gaze met hers placidly, so Kiara did her best to keep her voice calm.

"Why can I hear you?" she asked, swallowing the lump of emotion that formed in her throat.

Mage Stranglevine gave me to myself long before she died; I've always been able to speak with anyone I care to, unlike many of my kind.

Kiara nodded, and the thick knot of emotion eased some. She was touched that Gwen *wanted* to talk to her. Familiars were usually bound to the mage who had called them to this plane of existence, and at first when Gwen had spoken to her she'd wondered if it had meant something wonderful—or terrible. But she was happy to learn that Gwen could speak to whomever she chose and had chosen to speak to her.

"I'm honored you'd deign to speak to me, even still. And I wasn't aware that one could gift a familiar that kind of freedom. Is it common?"

Gwen sniffed in a catlike way that resembled scoffing.

I've never met another of my kind whose mage-friend had thought to try. Given how many mages think we are a power to be contained or a resource to be used, rather than people in our own right, I'm unsurprised by this.

Kiara nodded. It was, in fact, a large part of why she'd never tried to acquire a familiar of her own. Most mages with familiars went on and on about how the creatures from the ethereal plane would never have access to this plane of existence on their own, and how the ethereals' own pursuits of power and knowledge led them to agree to the deal to begin with. But to Kiara it had always seemed too one-sided a deal.

For one thing, familiars were bound solely to the mage who brought them over, so they were limited to whatever knowledge their mage decided to pursue. If their interests diverged from that of the mage they'd attached themselves to, they could do little about it. For another, familiars were bound by oaths to protect their mages, but their mages swore no such oath in return. This was always brushed aside (by the mages, at least) as being irrelevant, since any creature from the ethereal plane could restore themselves simply by returning to that plane of existence. They could heal from the most grievous, even mortal, injuries. But Kiara had known all her life that healing from pain was not the same as never feeling it to begin with.

"Well, I'm delighted that Mage Stranglevine figured out a way to let you have your freedom in this realm. I've never felt particularly good about the deal most mages make with their familiars," Kiara admitted.

If we found it completely disagreeable, it is not a bargain we would ever make. Most mages do not live very long compared to our kind, so the risks are manageable enough.

Kiara thought about that for a moment. With her elven heritage, she might expect to live for hundreds of years. There were mages who were also dragons—not many, because dragon magic worked so differently from mage spells, but there were some—and dragons lived for eons. But, yes, she supposed that even still, ethereal creatures lived many times that span.

"Now I'm not sure why you bother with us at all," she mused.

The people of this realm do interesting things with the short time given to them. And if we are very lucky, we find a companion like Mage Stranglevine, someone who understands what we truly are, and what our loyalty can accomplish without bonds.

Kiara swallowed at the implication of the ethereal's words, but before she could ask any clarifying questions another shriek tore through the forest.

Lyra!

The enormous panther sprinted away towards the shriek, and Kiara hurried to follow.

Chapter Seven
Check for Traps

Yra still wasn't certain what the vine creature actually *was*, but she could tell it was in trouble. The only sound she could hear now was its low keening whine, which was made extra eerie by the fact that up until she'd reached the strangely glowing clearing, there had been all the usual animal noises one would expect in a forest, even if they'd had a bit of a cursed-forest edge to them. Not only was the forest around this clearing silent, but even the vines from the trees had stopped trying to grab her once she'd gotten more than a few feet off the ground—allowing her the fastest climb she'd accomplished since entering this cursed place. When she finally situated herself in the middle of a wide branch fifty feet off the forest floor, and took a good look at what had earned her the reprieve, she wasn't sure it was worth the trade-off.

It appeared to be a massive spider web, if spiders wove their webs from light rather than silk, and wove them large enough to cover entire clearings more than twenty feet across.

The web clearly had the unmoving vine creature snared in its glow, but, curiously, Lyra didn't feel trapped, or compelled, or anything unusual really, so perhaps it didn't work from this distance? Or maybe it had something to do with the purplish cast to the light on this side of the web, whereas the light that filled the clearing was a pure golden glow? Of course, she couldn't be certain that the vine creature was truly ensnared by the web of light, but, given that it still wasn't moving even as a dozen enormous glowing spiders descended from where they had been hidden in the darkness above the clearing, Lyra felt it was a fairly safe bet.

Light spinners? She had thought those were more myth than reality, but here she was confronted with a dozen of them descending on the creature who held Gwen's pendant. And if any of the myths were to be believed, light spinners consumed magic.

"Well fuck," she breathed.

She didn't trust completely that the vine-covered… whatever it was… didn't mean her harm, but it hadn't harmed her yet or even tried to, unless you counted taking her pendant—but that had seemed more like bad luck than ill will. Regardless, even if it had stolen her pendant on purpose, that didn't mean it deserved to die a horrible death drained of all of its magic.

She figured it had to be at least somewhat magical, because she couldn't figure out how so many vines in such an odd shape could actually move without magical assistance. Even if Kiara was right, and the thing had been cursed to be covered in those vines, chances were good that whatever made it sentient *also* involved magic.

But whether or not the creature had magic of its own, the light spinners were surely drawn to Gwen's pendant, which, being the vessel and bond of a familiar from the ethereal plane, was actually more magic than it was mithril. In other words, it was one heck of a tasty snack for a hungry light spinner.

She had no idea what that might do to Gwen, and she wasn't about to find out.

Lyra took a few deep breaths and shook out her wrists. Her legs were loosely locked around the nice thick branch that was supporting her weight reassuringly.

She'd have to go about this carefully. She couldn't very well fight off a dozen light spinners by herself. They were each half the size of her, which meant that by sheer volume alone she was outnumbered six to one, but more than that, *she* was at least partially made of magic. The water magic that coursed through her might not be as tasty a snack as an ethereal pendant or a cursed vine creature, but it would be tasty enough that the light spinners were unlikely to ignore her, especially if she tried to steal their next meal.

So, for a moment, Lyra could only watch in horror as the light spinners dropped lower and lower and the vine creature continued to keen but otherwise didn't twitch a single vine. Even as the fastest of them shot forward and slowly looped what appeared to be threads of light secreted from its abdomen around the vine creature, all she could do was stare. The vine creature's keening intensified, but otherwise it did nothing to dissuade the giant arachnids that converged on it.

She didn't think the creature would die immediately when they finished wrapping it up; after all, that wasn't how most spiders operated. Lyra was no expert, but she thought spiders generally cocooned their victims first and *then* injected whatever venom they possessed to dissolve what was inside before finally sucking out the slurry that resulted sometime later. At least, that was how the little house spiders she allowed to remain in her home and café (and who in exchange kept the other creepy crawlies to a minimum) behaved. She could only hope that the light spinners worked in a similar fashion, but regardless she didn't think it was a good idea to let them finish wrapping the creature up. She *definitely* wanted to intervene before they had a chance to inject it with whatever they used to create their magic smoothie. She didn't like to think what effects that might have on the vine creature, or on Gwen's pendant when it came right down to it.

It pained Lyra to wait even a few more heartbeats, but if she didn't time this right she was going to die horribly, right along with the vine creature. Gwen would be furious with her—not that she'd ever hear about it since she'd be dead. But she hated the idea of leaving the enormous panther behind to mourn her. Or, worse, of leaving the panther trapped in the ethereal plane because her pendant got devoured by a horde of magic-eating spiders.

I would be both furious and sad all at once, and that is entirely too many emotions for me.

Lyra laughed in relief at the sound of Gwen's voice in her mind. *I take it you and Kiara made short work of those bugbear zombies?* she replied.

I don't know about 'short work', but they will not be getting up and moving again any time soon. The forest tore them into rather too many pieces for even the most stubborn undead to return from. I believe Kiara will be along shortly. She is not quite as fast as I am, poor dear.

Lyra suppressed a laugh, thinking it was grossly unfair to compare anyone's running speed to that of an enormous panther. Hells, a regular panther could easily outrun most two-legged people, but Gwen was a panther the size of a small elephant. She could cover distances so quickly that even when Lyra knew she wasn't shifting planes she still half suspected the panther was using a teleport spell.

"Well, we'll just have to muddle along as best we can 'til she gets here," Lyra muttered, her mouth quirked up to one side.

Now that Gwen was here, she felt a hundred times better about her chances of success. But she still needed to hurry if she didn't want the strange vine creature to get eaten.

I'm going to lure them away, Gwen. Can you cut the vine creature free if I do?

Gwen made her preferred scoffing noise—something between a hiss and sneeze—and Lyra almost laughed, but quickly sobered her expression.

They eat magic, Gwen. I'm worried it's one of the few kinds of damage that might cause you lasting injury. If you can't safely cut the creature away then we'll regroup and figure out a different plan.

I appreciate your concern, little one, I will not let them harm me… or you.

Lyra smiled, touched by the protective growl in the giant cat's voice—and then she fell over sideways and started screaming.

K IARA WAS SPRINTING through the cursed forest on four-inch stilettos, heaving breaths of damp air tinged with the faint rotten smell that accompanied most cursed forests, and questioning, if not her life choices, then at least her fashion sense. Thank all the gods that she had spelled these boots so the stiletto heels didn't stab into the earth with every step. Also, running on her toes like this was easier than running flat-footed would have been, especially given the sheer number of roots, vines, rocks, and fallen logs she had to jump as she followed the partially cleared path the vine creature had left. Unfortunately, the padding in these boots was non-existent, and, unlike all her other shoes, they didn't have a soft flexible sole that allowed her feet to flex and move freely. In short, she was going to have wicked blisters after this, and she half suspected that if she went to Est for healing, her best friend would just laugh at her for having tried to run in the damned things to begin with.

Not that this was the first time she'd had to run in the damned things, and it likely wouldn't be the last either. Some days she just wanted the flair of knee-high boots with dramatically sharp heels. She had even been known to wear them while adventuring, which was why she'd spelled them the way she had.

The bigger problem was that she didn't normally do this much running when she was adventuring. She was essentially a magical battering ram on two legs. Her job was to hold the enemy in place with overwhelming firepower while her teammates did all the work requiring finesse, dexterity, and subtlety. She was a blunt instrument. If a team didn't have a battle mage, they had a berserker or a paladin. They all ticked the same strategic box. And they did not, as a rule, *run*.

Which is why Kiara was a panting, blistered, sweaty mess. It was also why she was taking a short breather, her palms pressed against her knees as she tried desperately to extend her diaphragm and get more air into her heaving lungs.

Then she heard what was unmistakably the sound of Lyra screaming. Not the strange shriek of the vine creature, not some unknown animal in the woods making odd noises. Lyra. Screaming.

It was like her body found a reserve of energy that she'd been unable to access until that moment.

Without thinking, her spine straightened and her legs were pistoning beneath her. The obstacles on the path ahead seemed to cease existing, though she was dimly aware that she was using fire to incinerate anything that dared to get in her way. The ache and exhaustion that had suffused her body a heartbeat earlier had vanished, and she now moved with the grace of a panther.

Is this some spell I've accidentally cast on myself? she wondered. But she didn't have time to give it any more thought, as just then she stumbled headfirst into a clearing filled with a very odd light… and far too many spiders.

"COME AND GET ME YOU EIGHT-LEGGED EXO-THERMS! I'LL BASH YOUR CARAPACES TO DUST AND SHIT ON THE PIECES!"

Lyra had never hung upside down from a vine before while wildly swinging her arms and shouting invective at enormous spiders, and she wasn't sure she would add it to her list of preferred activities. Zero out of ten. Would not recommend to future cursed forest visitors.

She'd had to get creative with her invective after her initial war cry had done nothing to distract the twelve enormous spiders from their newest meal. She'd tried insulting their families, their ancestors, even their intelligence. None of it had done anything to draw their attention. Now she was just shouting facts as if they were insulting and following it up with threats. Which didn't seem to be working any better, if she was being honest.

Of course, she'd mostly assumed that the spiders would shift their attention to her because she was another source of magic and thus food for them. But, apparently, she offered too little nutrition when compared with the vine creature they were slowly enveloping with threads of light on the forest floor.

She lobbed another illumination spell into the air above the spiders in hopes of drawing their attention with her magic.

"I AM A TASTY SNACK!" she screamed, following up the illumination spell with a heat spell she mostly used for drying clothes in winter.

She was afraid to use anything resembling an offensive spell against the enormous spiders. They were all clustered around the vine creature and, consequently, Gwen's pendant, so her odds of missing the spiders and damaging the vine creature and pendant were entirely too high for her liking.

Unfortunately, her displays of light and heat were no more effective at drawing them away than her shouting had been, and she was going to have to change tactics soon if—

Something burst into the clearing at high speed, immediately tripped over a log, and fell over, crushing at least three of the light spinners beneath it.

The shrieks from the light spinners, either of agony or surprise (Lyra couldn't tell), made her ears hurt, and she watched in horror and awe as the nine remaining spiders turned on the thing that had killed their friends.

Which was, of course, Kiara.

"I IGHT SPINNERS? I thought you'd gone extinct," Kiara said to the clearing at large as she stood and brushed bits of crushed spider from her greatcoat with a few tidy flicks of her sleeves.

Though she was still rather awkwardly hanging upside down from a vine a few dozen feet off the ground, Lyra took one brief moment to appreciate the sheer amount of spellcraft that must have gone into that greatcoat—it shed spider ichor as easily as her rain boots shed water! Then she remembered that she'd been in the midst of a carefully timed distraction.

A distraction that Kiara had just ruined.

But Lyra knew that Gwen was nothing if not adaptable, and indeed, as soon as the remaining nine light spinners started closing ranks on Kiara, Gwen began her stealthy approach towards the half-cocooned mass of vines that still held her pendant.

Lyra quickly realized that with Kiara now playing the part of "magical snack that also happened to kill your friends" her own role in this half-cocked retrieval plan was now a bit more flexible.

She eyed the vine creature and could see Gwen's quick claws already flicking out to sever the threads of light that cocooned it.

Lyra had no idea how one severed threads of light, but it was clear that Gwen could handle it on her own.

It was less clear if Kiara would be able to fend off nine enormous spiders who ate magic.

Indeed, Kiara was already backpedaling around the edge of the clearing with her hands up in a "I mean no trouble" position. Lyra couldn't tell how much of that was an attempt to get the spiders farther away from Gwen and the cocoon (which would be smart), and how much of it was Kiara actually hoping to dissuade the light spinners from attacking. Lyra was a bit surprised the battle mage hadn't started lobbing fireballs already, but she had to assume a seasoned adventurer like Kiara knew better than to throw magic at something that would just eat it.

So Lyra waited a few more beats, did the kind of sit up that she wished someone had witnessed (because honestly, while it didn't look flashy, pulling her body upright, or in this case perpendicular, from hanging upside down always felt like a godsdamned act of heroism) and then wrapped her hands around the vine that held her, released her legs from their wrap, and dropped towards the forest floor at speed.

K IARA WAS BEGINNING to regret carelessly crashing into this clearing. At first, she had only seen that there were spiders and something large trapped in a cocoon. She'd been half-convinced the trapped thing was Lyra, because why else had she heard the woman screaming? So she'd panicked like a new recruit and gone sprinting into danger without any kind of plan.

There was an odd golden glow to this clearing and, even though she could sense the darkness of the cursed forest around the edges of it, she felt as though the golden light suffused everything now, as though the world might have narrowed to this golden circle full of deadly spiders and nothing existed beyond its bounds. Weirdly, she thought she could smell traces of Est's best healing salve, or maybe the waybread her grandfather used to make before their excursions into the wilds of Tyrfalyn. That was odd, considering how she should probably just smell forest floor and whatever it was giant spiders smelled like.

"Stupid, stupid, stupid," she muttered as she continued to back away from the glowing monstrosities who had clearly not taken the deaths of their three friends well.

She must have been doing something right, though, because Gwen's voice had murmured, *Keep them distracted,* in her head as soon as she'd stood up from the pile of crushed spiders she'd accidentally created upon entering the clearing. Even now, in her peripheral vision, she could see Gwen was doing… something… to the strange cocoon of light on the other side of the clearing.

Also, don't look up, Gwen had added. So Kiara had kept her hands up and continued backing away slowly from the nine spiders who were trying to close ranks on her.

The spiders weren't attacking her directly yet, and she knew better than to fire any spells at them. They'd only eat it and get stronger. Or, at least, that's what the textbooks said; she'd never actually fought a light spinner herself.

"Where is a sword swinger when you need one?" she asked no one in particular.

Which was when she heard a strange hissing noise coming from above her and getting closer by the second. Not wanting to be surprised by a spider landing on her (or worse), she made a potentially fatal mistake; she looked up.

At first, relief flooded through her. Lyra was alive, descending from a thick green vine like a forest goddess again, albeit a forest goddess who seemed to be in a bit of a hurry…

Was it safe for her to be descending that quickly? Surely not.

But before Kiara could do more than *begin* to worry about Lyra's speedy descent, her eyes caught on the golden glow behind Lyra. A brief warning screamed in her mind, but it was too late. She angled her head to look fully at the soft golden light, breathed in a deep lungful of air suffused with the scent of Est's best healing balm, and then she felt nothing at all.

YRA COULD SEE the moment that Kiara's consciousness fled her, and if she hadn't been about to let go of her vine anyway, it could have been a very bad moment indeed.

She hadn't meant to focus on the battle mage's face so intently. Hells, the whole reason she'd been looking down at all was to aim herself at the spiders properly and make sure she wasn't going to splat the mage when she landed. But the warm smile of relief, and—was it longing?—that had softened Kiara's features when she'd first looked up had stolen all of Lyra's attention.

So, she'd had nothing to distract her from watching Kiara's eyes go vacant and her smile go slack the moment she'd shifted her gaze slightly beyond Lyra.

Probably that damned web, Lyra theorized.

Lyra had heard Gwen's warning not to look up, a thought the ethereal panther had directed at both Lyra and Kiara, but Lyra hadn't fully understood the warning at the time. She'd already been looking "up" from where she'd been perched on her branch, and that hadn't proven dangerous. At least, not that she'd noticed.

Now that she'd seen Kiara's expression turn vacant, she was forming her own theory about what they shouldn't be looking at, but she wasn't about to test it now.

The moment the battle mage's expression had blanked, her arms had dropped limply to her sides. Yet, oddly, Kiara's legs seemed to remain firm beneath her, even as the light spinners had quickly pinned her in with their bulbous, glowing bodies.

Or, they would have, if that hadn't been the exact moment Lyra had plummeted to the ground and squished three more of their number by aiming her impact-reducing tumble as carefully as if she'd been bowling for spiders.

She hated that she was essentially murdering an endangered species, but they were clearly planning to kill her… her… Lyra fumbled for the appropriate label for what Kiara was to her, exactly. Her friend? They'd just met. They probably needed more time to become friends in any real sense of the word. Her potential girlfriend? That probably wasn't a thing. And even if it was, it probably wasn't accurate because there was no way a hardened battle mage was ever going to be able to put up with how broken Lyra was, no matter how much Kiara seemed to understand grief. Well, they were planning to kill *her date*, at any rate, and Lyra didn't care how doomed their future non-relationship was; she drew the line at letting her date get eaten by magic spiders.

When she rose from her tumble, she found that she finally had the spiders' undivided attention. This made her particularly glad that there were only six of them now.

She was also glad that Kiara had, however inadvertently, revealed that they were physically pretty fragile, at least when it came to getting crushed. There was probably a good way to use that in a fight. *I mean, we've already used it against them twice, right? That has to count for something.*

Unfortunately, as the remaining six spiders closed in on her and she took stock of what vines she could reach from here, she became distinctly aware that she was still completely and utterly fucked.

"LOOK, IT'S NOT that I'm not magical, it's just that… I'm a hearth witch. I probably taste like dirty socks and the things that rot in the back corners of ice boxes, you know? Or maybe I taste like vinegar and mops, but still… not exactly appetizing, right?"

Lyra had her hands up and was backing away from the spiders, just as Kiara had been doing (before she'd been ensnared by the light web) but Lyra wasn't going to make the mistake of looking up.

She hoped.

She was keeping very careful track of her footing to make sure she didn't just trip over a root, look at the light web, and save the spiders the trouble of having to drive their pincers into her, or whatever it was they did to victims they hadn't been able to wrap in a cocoon first. Luckily, in this eerily silent clearing bathed in golden light, there didn't seem to be nearly as many roots, rocks, or slithering vines as there had been out in the rest of the cursed forest. In fact, now that she thought about it, it was kind of strange that Kiara had managed to trip over what seemed to be the only fallen log in the entire clearing. Lyra supposed that had to count as a lucky break, since it had not only distracted the light spinners from devouring the poor vine creature, but had also demonstrated just how susceptible the enormous spiders were to being crushed.

When she'd first started the speedy descent she'd used to take out three more light spinners, Lyra had been hopeful that her attack might give them the chance to escape and take the cocooned vine creature with them somehow. But now that she was on the ground, alone, confronted with six spiders that were each half as big as she was, and no battle mage to back her up, she was at a loss for what else she could do to them. Hells, she didn't even have a good spider-killing spell for *non*-magical arachnids because she was very much on team "gently set the spider outside if it's bothering you, or else let it hang out and eat all your other bugs."

"You know, I don't usually kill spiders," she said, wondering if that was at all helpful to her case. "I generally really appreciate any spiders that are willing to hang out in my home and help keep the fly population down, you know?"

But, apparently, "I don't usually kill spiders, but I made an exception for your friends just now," was not the argument in her favor that she'd been hoping for. The light spinners pressed in on her, their mandibles extended menacingly and their legs scuttling forward without hesitation.

It was only when she'd done close to a full lap around the clearing that she realized the spiders didn't seem to have any real attack planned. They seemed to be waiting for her to stumble, or look up for no reason, or maybe get distracted, at which point she supposed they would all jump on her and try to inject her with venom or something.

Of course, she could turn and run away from the clearing and into the forest, hoping to outrun them, and she probably *would*. If they were actually faster than she was, they undoubtedly would have launched themselves at her already.

Like most web hunting spiders, they likely played a waiting game with their prey and relied on patience and traps.

They weren't jumping spiders, or spitting spiders, thank all the gods, so maybe all she had to do was keep them busy until Gwen was finished with… whatever it was the ethereal panther was doing. (Lyra had thought she was simply cutting the vine creature out of its cocoon, but Gwen had leapt up into the trees a good minute ago, and the vine creature hadn't even twitched despite its newfound freedom.) Maybe as soon as Gwen was done they could grab Kiara and the vine creature and run.

"Did I ever tell you about the time my Aunt Violet stumbled into a whole nest of basilisks?" she asked conversationally, hoping to give Gwen whatever time she needed.

L YRA WAS STILL walking backwards, monologuing like a petty villain, and just starting to feel like she could keep up this whole "distract the magic-eating spiders for as long as Gwen needs you" thing, when she heard a low growl above her and almost turned her head to look.

She caught herself just in time, and fortunately, managed to keep her eyes on the spiders that surged around her.

Unfortunately, the aborted motion of glancing away threw off her balance and, while she was generally graceful enough to recover from a small shift like that, her heel chose that exact moment to collide with a root, which turned out to be one overbalance too many.

She went down hard on her ass and slid through several layers of grass and fallen leaves, only to find a layer of damp moss soaking her into her clothes.

Luckily, she was too distracted by the murderous spiders leaping at her face to worry about how the moss would probably make it look like she'd pissed herself. Hells, she might even go ahead and piss herself for real, because she could not think of a single damned spell that would stop her from dying horribly in the next thirty seconds.

She raised her arms in front of her, as if the spiders would somehow be less likely to inject her arms with venom than her face—an inane thought if ever she'd had one—and wished she knew some kind of shield spell that was impervious to magic eaters. But, given that a spell being impervious to magic eaters was a contradiction in terms, she resorted to kicking wildly with her legs as she fell back, doing her best to keep the spiders away. Yet, despite feeling her feet connect with something hard and chitinous a few times, she could tell she wasn't doing anything but pissing the spiders off more.

Now that she was on her back, she couldn't even risk a glance between her arms, because she was just as likely to wind up ensnared in the light spinners' web as gain any insights about how to defend herself. More likely, she would just get a much better look at how she was about to die before catching sight of the web and doing most of the light spinners' work for them.

Which was why she had no way to see the zombie bugbears breaking into the clearing before they arrived.

And though she heard them as they attacked the first of the spiders that had surrounded her, she didn't risk sitting up and opening her eyes until she'd gone a full ten seconds without a set of pincers trying to snag any part of her body. When she was certain she was no longer pointed towards the glowing web and finally cracked her eyes open, she nearly sagged with relief.

The spiders, unsurprisingly, had turned immediately on the bigger threat.

They were being summarily crushed by the club-wielding bugbear zombies. There were only two bugbears at the moment, but she wasn't in any way convinced that more wouldn't show up in short order, so Lyra decided not to waste this rather perfect distraction. She fumbled to her feet and ran to Kiara's unmoving form.

KIARA SAW GOLDEN light, smelled her grandfather's waybread, and felt nothing.

Or rather, she felt everything. Everything was light and golden magic. There was nothing for her to worry about. Nothing to think about. Nothing that her mind needed to do but bask in the warm golden glow and be at peace.

But something was tugging at her.

That was odd. And unpleasant. The golden light was perfection. Basking in it brought peace. For the first time in her life, she was certain that there was nothing that needed her attention. If she simply remained here, unmoving, all would be well. The golden glow would protect her from everything, and she would be one with magic.

One with everything.

That was the promise of the golden glow.

Except that her peace was being ruined by whatever was pulling on her arm. There was no sound within the golden glow, nothing but the sound of peace filling her entire being… but it did seem that there was a faraway voice saying the same word over and over again.

It couldn't possibly be important, that voice. Nor could the distant sensation of tugging on her arm… but it was relentless. She tried to shake off the tugging. It stopped for a moment, and Kiara returned, blissfully, to the golden glow and the peace that came with it.

Sometime later (she wasn't certain how long it had been; time was not a thing she had to worry about anymore), she thought she heard a voice close to her. And though there was no sound within the golden glow, she thought she might have heard something vaguely like the word "Sorry."

And then something struck her very hard across the face.

"Ow," muttered Kiara.

Lyra nearly sobbed with relief.

Standing in the golden glow and the eerie silence of the clearing, a silence now broken by the sounds of bugbears squashing light spinners and light spinners hissing for reinforcements (at least, that's what Lyra assumed was happening, she wasn't all that interested in checking), was absolutely not an experience that Lyra wanted to keep up for a single second longer. Even the faint smell of her aunt's favorite saddle soap that permeated the clearing (for unclear and probably horrible reasons) was not enough to comfort her against the sounds of bugbears and giant spiders doing battle behind her.

But yelling at Kiara about bugbears and imminent death hadn't done a damned thing to snap the battle mage out of her trance.

Lyra had tried pinching her arm first because sometimes pain was the only thing that could break a good trance, but it hadn't been enough.

Lyra had briefly considered punching the battle mage, but she wasn't certain she wouldn't just wind up breaking her own hand. She'd tried slapping her open-handed, but that had done nothing to shake her from whatever the light spinners' web had done to her either.

In the end, she'd had to trust her great uncle's sturdiest cast iron with the job. She'd apologized in advance and really hoped that she wouldn't wind up giving the battle mage a concussion. But Lyra was certain concussions could be healed. Having your magic eaten by giant spiders seemed a lot harder to treat.

She'd dithered for a full minute, while the giant spiders were falling rapidly to the zombified bugbears, and ultimately decided that she really did not want to still be standing there tugging uselessly at Kiara's wrist when the bugbears started looking for their next target.

Luckily, the cast iron had worked. Now she just had to hope the woman would forgive her once she'd had a chance to explain.

"More bugbear zombies, no time to explain, we've got to get out of here and we need to bring the vine creature with us."

Kiara blinked at her very slowly and then managed a nod.

"Where is… Gwen?" the battle mage asked after a few blinks.

"Busy. Let's collect the vine creature."

Lyra didn't have time to explain what Gwen was up to, but even more, she didn't want to risk telling Kiara about it.

After all, the battle mage had just spent however many minutes trapped by the light web above them, and had no intention of directing her attention towards that magical trap again anytime soon.

"This way," said Lyra, grabbing Kiara by the hand and towing her along like a confused life raft.

Lyra did her best to ignore the small frisson of heat that flicked up her arm when she grabbed the battle mage. She was just trying to get the woman to safety; it didn't have to mean anything.

Besides, Kiara had just come out of a trance; she might as well be drugged, and Lyra was absolutely NOT going to take advantage of someone whose thoughts had been scattered like dandelion fluff in a strong wind. She was just being efficient, and keeping them both from dying horribly, by making sure that Kiara didn't wander off in the wrong direction.

She tried to smother the thought that, if they *did* make it out of this mess alive, she might have to see how the whole hand-holding thing worked out—because her body was definitely responding to this very simple physical activity in a way that seemed a tad excessive.

Sylvan is right, she thought, *I really need to get out more. I should not be this turned on by holding a woman's hand.*

Of course, Lyra was fairly certain that she wouldn't be this turned on if the woman in question hadn't been Kiara. After all, it wasn't like Kiara was the first woman she'd touched since her last breakup. She might not have held out any hope for romance, but she'd gone out dancing with her troupe friends enough times to enjoy the physical affection of a handful of women in the past few years. None of them had made her nerves sing the way Kiara did.

But she's a battle mage, and you're a broken mess who no one has the patience to deal with, so why don't you just let it go, her own voice whispered inside her head.

Then she reminded herself that they were stuck in a cursed forest and they could only get out by working together. So she ignored the little voice and didn't let go of Kiara's hand, even when they reached the part of the clearing that held the vine creature.

Kiara only blinked blankly at the thing for a few moments before finally asking, "What do I do?"

Lyra couldn't tell if the sound building up in her throat was a laugh or a scream. It wasn't that she didn't have sympathy for the battle mage just having taken old uncle Serysis' best cast iron upside the head; it was just that they were probably going to die very soon if they didn't get moving.

"Do you have some magical means of bringing the vine creature along with us? While it's entranced? Gwen managed to cut it free from the light cocoon, but I can still see her pendant sticking out from its… whatever that is… actually from here it kind of looks like a mouth? Or a lid? Anyway, I think getting the pendant away might be tricky. So, we should get it away from here so it doesn't get eaten by spiders, or killed by bugbears, which… which seem to keep chasing it for reasons that are honestly… do you… Why do you think the bugbears are after this thing anyway?"

Lyra belatedly realized that a good portion of that little speech had probably made no sense. Her questions were a jumble that had started off coherent enough in her mind, but then she'd done the thing she often did, where she answered her own question in the middle of asking it, and then started on a new question immediately after. Poor Kiara was already looking a bit lost after being caught in that web, not to mention getting hit with a frying pan, and Lyra really should have waited to ask all of that because none of it mattered except for getting the vine creature to safety.

So she tried again.

"Can we move the vine creature somehow?"

Kiara blinked a few more times and then said, "I think if we move it before it's out of the trance it might turn violent. Or even if it's not, we might wind up stripping it of whatever consciousness it has. That web did NOT want to let me go and I think if I'd realized what you were doing before you'd hit me with… whatever that was, I'd have tried to hurt you."

Lyra did not like the sound of that, but she also didn't find it particularly surprising.

The light spinners probably didn't care much what happened to their food if it tried to get away. If anything, they'd *want* it to turn into a mindless husk that just sat there waiting for them to devour it.

"Right. Well, any ideas on how we can get it out of the trance before we all get eaten by bugbears?"

She just barely resisted the urge to turn and look over her shoulder, but she didn't want to attract the zombified bugbears' attention, or risk looking up and getting caught in the light web. For now, the bugbears seemed content bashing spiders, but that wasn't guaranteed to last, and as curious as Lyra was about *why* the bugbears wanted the damned vine creature so badly, she was far more interested in surviving this date, getting Gwen's pendant back, and then getting the hells out of here.

Kiara seemed to be very carefully not looking up, and when she spoke she only pointed towards the canopy above them, while directing her eyes firmly at the ground.

"I think we'll have to—"

But whatever Kiara thought they would have to do was cut off by a triumphant roar as the clearing went dark and the light spinners evaporated into dust.

"WELL, THAT MAKES this easier in some ways," Kiara muttered as she lunged forward and grabbed the writhing mass of tentacle-like vines they had been chasing for the past hour. "And harder in others."

Kiara's mind had cleared considerably the moment that the clearing had gone dark, and she had known with utter certainty that the light web had been destroyed, even before Gwen's triumphant roar had rung out from above. Even after Lyra had hit her and somehow released the golden web's hold on her, Kiara's thoughts had still been muddled and far away, as though her brain had been on loan to someone else and the thoughts had needed to travel a very long distance from her body to her brain and back again. The moment the light web had been extinguished, it was as though her mind had been fully returned to her body. She still had a headache, and likely would for a while yet thanks to whatever Lyra had been forced to hit her with earlier, but that could be healed—as long as they could make it back to Dryvenvale.

Thankfully, she wasn't feeling dizzy. She hoped that meant her movement wouldn't be impaired.

But, regardless of how well balanced she was, now that the web had gone dark they didn't have time to ask the vine creature politely to come with them and wait for its reply, because there were some very angry bugbear zombies behind them who had just been deprived of their eight-legged punching bags and who, if the stomping footsteps behind them were anything to judge by, had already noticed that two more potential punching bags were making off with a third punching bag (which the bugbears had, for whatever reason, been chasing since Kiara and Lyra had arrived).

Kiara didn't wait to see how close the bugbears were getting before she started running, or waddling as quickly as she could with a mass of vines overflowing from her arms and partially blocking her view. She could just make out that Lyra was running along with her through the jumble of green.

"Gwen?" Kiara asked no one in particular, unsure if she was expecting Gwen to answer for herself, or if she hoped that Lyra would know where the enormous panther was now.

Right behind you, just delaying these zombies a bit.

Lyra and Kiara didn't stop to find out what Gwen meant by that. The panther could clearly take care of herself. Their job was to keep running.

Of course, they'd only made it a few strides out of the clearing when the vine creature started to struggle. Kiara could hardly blame it, since it hadn't been asked for its consent before they picked it up and carried it off, but you'd think a creature that had been fleeing from zombie bugbears all day might appreciate that it was still moving away from them without even having to twitch its vines.

"Aaah!" Lyra shouted, as a rogue vine flapped aggressively in her face.

Kiara tried to adjust the massive bundle of vines and… whatever else this thing was… she couldn't tell much about it aside from the fact that it weighed as much as she did… but, adjusting her grip did next to nothing. She could barely get her arms far enough around the thing to hold it off the ground. There really wasn't much she could do to restrain it without throwing a net over it, and taking the time to do that would get them eaten by zombie bugbears, so that rather defeated the purpose.

She could hear the zombie bugbears behind them struggling with Gwen, even over the sounds of her and Lyra's feet thudding against the forest floor.

They were nowhere near the trail they'd started on—after their wild chase behind the vine creature—and when they'd left the clearing, they hadn't stopped to find the path it had cut, so now they were just plowing through the thick underbrush of the cursed forest. Which meant the underbrush was just one more thing trying to kill them, and the bugbears were likely to catch up to them when they inevitably had to stop to detangle themselves from the roots and vines snaring them. *Too late to do anything about that now.* So they just kept running and hoped that by the time the forest stopped them they'd be far enough away from the bugbears that it wouldn't make a difference.

As she pounded through the dark forest, with a struggling vine creature taking up most of her field of vision and a curvy café owner running behind her and occasionally pulling the more tenacious vines off of her arms, neck and shoulders, Kiara began to wonder if the other woman was completely horrified by this whole adventure yet. Lyra'd done remarkably well for someone who didn't regularly fight monsters, but Kiara had to assume that she was going to start regretting this entire experience very soon. After all, if she really wanted this much excitement in her life she would have joined the Adventurer's Guild herself. She wouldn't be running a cozy coffee shop and going on dates with a matchmaking service. Right?

Kiara shook herself and tried to focus on where to put her feet that wouldn't get her snagged by a cursed vine, rather than how well Lyra might or might not be taking the risks of adventuring. After all, what did Kiara care if Lyra was putting up with getting attacked by zombie bug-bears well? Just because Lyra could stand a little mortal peril when she didn't have any other choice didn't mean that she was going to be miraculously ok with dating someone whose job required them to court mortal peril all the time—especially when Lyra was clearly still reeling from the death of her aunt.

Mage Stranglevine had died defending a small village located somewhere west of nowhere that had been under attack from a very persistent Lich Queen, and that could not possibly have increased Lyra's inclination to build a life with someone whose job was exactly as risky as her late aunt's.

If anything, Lyra was even less likely to be ok with Kiara's chosen profession than Evain had been.

It was somewhere in the middle of this train of thought that Kiara tripped over a root, or possibly one of the vine creatures' flailing limbs. It was difficult to tell, since most of her vision was filled with flailing vines, and it was too dark to discern which vines were which. But no matter what had tripped her, the result was the same: she and the vine creature both went tumbling full speed onto the forest floor.

YRA, WHO HAD been keeping as close as she could to Kiara, tripped over the whole mess.

They landed in a heap of limbs and vines, and the creature startled and let out another one of its shrieks. Lyra could barely figure out where Kiara ended and the vine creature began, but in that moment she caught sight of a flash of silver, and when she focused on it she could see the panther figurine that was Gwen's pendant. She reached out for it without thinking, before she'd even had a chance to disentangle herself from the writhing mess, and that was when the vine creature opened what appeared to be an enormous mouth.

Lyra shrank back before she could touch the pendant, but Kiara chose that moment to try to stand up, which, due to the way that various vines and limbs were entangled, shoved Lyra forward into the glowing opening that the pendant had been dangling from. Lyra fell, and before she could even sort out which direction she was falling, (down, the answer was down, but it hadn't really felt like it at first) she found herself completely enveloped by the glow that she'd seen from the creature's… mouth?

"LYRA!"

She heard Kiara scream her name, but she couldn't do anything about it. She couldn't stop herself from falling, and she wasn't even sure she could gather the air to breathe. What did Kiara think shouting her name would accomplish?

But just as she was sinking further into the glow, Lyra felt something catch her ankle. For a moment she thought that Kiara had caught her, that the battle mage would be able to pull her out to safety. Instead, a heartbeat later, she felt herself pitch forward even faster and when she finally hit bottom—a very lumpy, painful, not at all evenly distributed bottom—a loud clanking thud followed behind her.

"What the hells..." She blinked a few times and the space around her took shape, though it wasn't a shape she could make much sense of.

"I think we just got swallowed by a cursed chest," said Kiara's voice beside her.

Chapter Eight
Cursed Chest

LYRA LOOKED AROUND the cavernous space they'd fallen into and wondered if her brain had simply given up on reality and decided to throw her into a dream instead. She couldn't actually see the walls of wherever they were, nor could she see the ceiling or floor. She was sitting on piles of treasure—all kinds, really, but mostly gold—and she could see nothing but mounds of treasure all around her. It was largely her nose that convinced her she wasn't actually dreaming. The smells of the forest were completely gone, replaced with a tang of metal in the air, and possibly something like armor polish or incense.

"I can't believe that weird tangle of vines was actually a cursed chest this entire time," Kiara complained.

"How do you know it was a cursed chest?" Lyra asked, grateful for the distraction.

"Because we are inside what is clearly a pocket dimension, and this is a lot of valuable loot."

Lyra couldn't really argue with that. The space they were in was filled with a golden glow that was completely unlike the golden glow of the light spinners' web. This was the glow of light reflecting off of gold, and they were perched on piles of the stuff. Some of it was coins, some of it was crowns, some of it looked like expensive and heavily enchanted items. Not all of it was strictly gold, she supposed, but damned if she could tell the difference. She had no idea where the light itself was coming from. She couldn't see so much as a candle from where she was sitting.

She took a deep breath and shook out her wrists, then turned to the purple-eyed battle mage and asked the question her mind had started screaming soon as she'd fallen into this place, but which she had been far too afraid to ask aloud.

"Ok... so... how do we get out?"

Lyra didn't have much use for gold. I mean, sure she could grab a handful of this stuff and buy her coffee shop property outright, and maybe that was a good idea, but the words "cursed chest" made her think that grabbing any of the gold was a terrible idea. She had zero interest in *dying* for gold, or even remaining trapped for any amount of time in exchange for gold. Really, she would be delighted to just get back to her shop to tell Sylvan that this whole "dragon dating thing" wasn't safe for any of her customers and be done with it. She'd find a different way to help her shop, or maybe she'd just retire from the coffee shop business and pursue dancing as her sole career. Kyle seemed to make it work; maybe she should learn from him.

"We don't," said Kiara in a voice that Lyra *really* did not find reassuring. "It's a pocket dimension. You can't get out of it without getting grabbed on the other side and pulled free."

"What!? Why did you follow me in here then?" she asked, her heart thumping so loudly she was worried everyone else could hear it too.

"I was trying to grab your ankle to pull you out, but the damned chest used one of its vine legs to sweep me up and push me in after you instead," Kiara replied, sounding decidedly bitter.

Lyra took a few more deep breaths and then tried to focus on the upside.

"But... but... ok. No need to panic; Gwen will be able to pull us out of here once she catches up to the vine creature... cursed chest... whatever it is."

"Maybe, if she manages to get hold of her pendant first, and then finds a way to secure herself so that the chest can't push her in with us, like it did me."

Lyra very carefully didn't snap at Kiara that she was just trying to ruin Lyra's sense of calm.

"I mean, she's nine hundred pounds of feline fury," she reassured herself instead. "I think the chest would have a hard time putting her anywhere she doesn't want to be."

"True, but first she'll have to get her own pendant. She has to make sure that her anchor to our realm is IN our realm, or else she'll risk getting sucked into this pocket dimension just from touching her pendant and... *shit...*"

Kiara had cut herself off when she turned and looked to a spot a few feet past where Lyra was sitting on a bed of random treasures. Lyra did not want to turn and look at whatever it was the mage had just noticed, because Kiara's face told her that she was not going to like whatever she saw there, but she turned anyway... and saw Gwen's pendant lying at the top of the nearest pile of gold.

"Oh fuck," Lyra whispered.

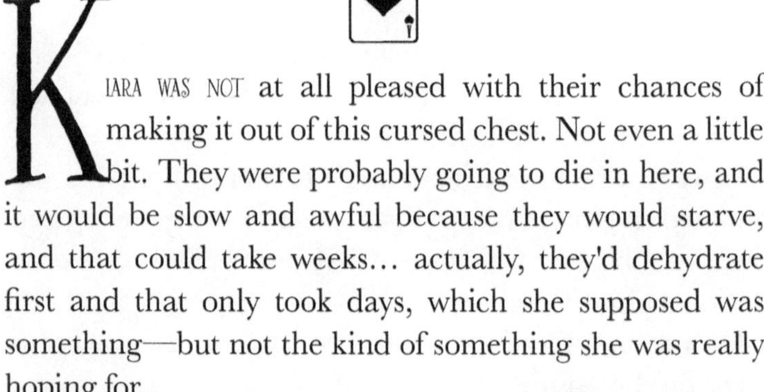

KIARA WAS NOT at all pleased with their chances of making it out of this cursed chest. Not even a little bit. They were probably going to die in here, and it would be slow and awful because they would starve, and that could take weeks... actually, they'd dehydrate first and that only took days, which she supposed was something—but not the kind of something she was really hoping for.

"Me either," muttered Lyra, whose skin had paled considerably, giving Kiara the first hint that she'd mumbled at least a portion of her last thought out loud.

Whoops. She was the experienced adventurer here. She needed to try not to lose her shit. Panicking wouldn't help anyone, and if *she* panicked Lyra had no reason not to panic too. She was used to being in these situations with fellow Guild members. Her crew was very experienced, and it had been years since the last time she'd needed to calm down a new recruit, or even just keep her cool so that no one else lost theirs.

Kiara cleared her throat.

"Umm... maybe it's not all bad? I mean, for one thing we get a break from running from bugbears, right? And... none of this treasure is trying to strangle us, or drag us under the forest floor or up a tree, so that's something, right? Also... I don't know... I probably have a bit of food in this cloak. Hang on..."

With an enthusiasm that was probably unwarranted, Kiara started the surprisingly time-consuming, and blissfully distracting, process of going through all the pockets in her greatcoat. There were... possibly hundreds of them.

She wasn't 100% sure. It had *come* with a LOT of pockets, as it was designed for adventuring mages, and then she'd magically added quite a few more pockets over the years. In fact, now that she began poking around, she was fairly certain there were some pockets she hadn't opened in almost a decade.

She knew that none of them were dangerous—to her, at least. Any of the pockets she'd trapped couldn't be triggered by her, and the rest were meant to be useful rather than destructive. Even still, not wanting to take too long in reassuring Lyra that she had at least *some* food, she carefully stuck to rummaging through the areas she thought were most likely to contain rations and tried to leave everything else in its place. Of course, her memory wasn't perfect, and some of the pocket spells had degraded a bit over time, but she only wound up pulling out a small pile of spell grenades and void bombs as she went.

She'd gotten through at least ten pockets without finding more than a lone piece of dried venison when she finally looked up from the inside of her coat and noticed that Lyra had laid out a smallish tablecloth that was now covered in pastries, cheeses, and something that looked suspiciously like an olive spread.

"I've also got hummus in here somewhere," Lyra said, reaching into what appeared to be a bag of holding, given how far her arm had disappeared into it relative to the size of the bag.

"You have a picnic," Kiara whispered, in a mixture of surprise and awe, as she slowly ceased turning her own pockets inside out.

"I mean, it's not much. I always have cheese and preserved olives in here, because they don't go bad and make excellent snacks. As for the rest, when we don't sell all of our pastries at the shop, Sylvan and I usually split them and give them to the neighborhood kids on our way home, so... we might as well eat them?"

"Should we… umm… wait to eat them later?"

Kiara did not particularly want to think, or remind Lyra, about how much later they would wish they had food. Nor did she wish to calculate how long they could make this food last, especially since it only seemed like delaying the inevitable.

"Well, we could wait… but, I've got enough cheese in here to last us a month, easy. And while we'll be thoroughly tired of cheese by then, we won't be dead. And unless my magic doesn't work down here, I can conjure enough water to keep us from dying of dehydration. I've got more than one scouring spell that sources water from a spring near the cabin where I grew up, and that thing isn't going dry anytime soon, so... it's simple enough to redirect the spell into drinking water. I don't see why we can't just enjoy the pastries now, before they get stale, and then see if we get any brilliant ideas about how to get out of here once we've eaten."

Lyra smiled almost sheepishly, as if she might be embarrassed to derail Kiara's pessimistic worries. Then she produced a small jug of water from the same bag and placed it on the tablecloth beside everything else.

Kiara didn't know what to say—there were far too many thoughts clamoring for attention at once—so she simply nodded, cut herself a bit of cheese from one of the hunks of aged cheddar Lyra had provided, and picked up a scone. Then she chewed the cheese thoughtfully, wondering if, now that it seemed they weren't going to starve in here, it was wrong of her to be happy that they'd both been swallowed by the cursed chest.

L YRA BROKE OFF pieces of her cheese and onion scone, dipped them into the olive spread she'd made a week ago, and wondered why she wasn't more upset that she was probably going to die in here with a battle mage she hardly knew.

Maybe because her death hardly seemed imminent. In fact, given how much food Lyra had access to through her bag of holding and a few of her sourcing spells, it wasn't likely they would starve in here for a *very* long time.

Maybe she wasn't concerned because she was confident they could figure out how to get out of here before anything permanently terrible happened to them; or maybe she was just so relieved to find herself no longer dodging bugbears and light spinners that she couldn't even process the looming threat of death by starvation inside of a cursed chest?

She let her eyes drift around the surprisingly vast, treasure-filled space as she swallowed another bite of scone dipped in olive spread.

"Do you suppose the bugbears were after this thing for the treasure?" she asked, once she'd finished the last of her scone. She reached for another one without much thought. She'd had an even dozen to take back to the neighborhood kids after they'd closed up shop, and that wasn't even counting the half-dozen cinnamon buns and croissants that hadn't quite sold out either. It had been a bit of a slow day for pastry sales, perhaps because of the weather. The pastries never did sell as well when it was hot out.

"What?" Kiara asked, snapping Lyra back to the present.

Lyra felt the battle mage's attention fix on her and a small flush crept into her neck and cheeks. Maybe she wasn't worried about dying in here with a strange battle mage because she was more than a little curious what she might learn about the woman now that they had time to talk without running away from mortal peril every five seconds.

"I said, do you think—"

"Oh, no, I heard you, I just... I'd kind of forgotten that the bugbears were chasing this thing before we even followed it. You're right though, that *is* odd. Maybe they were after the treasure, but... even live bugbears don't have much use for gold... What would undead bugbears want with it?"

"That's what I'm wondering," Lyra explained. "But, I mean, it wouldn't be *them* wanting what's inside the chest, would it? It would more likely be whatever was turning them into zombies, don't you think?"

"Hmm... that's assuming that someone consciously turned them into zombies. In this cursed forest, I honestly half expected them to be the victims of some strange slime mold or something."

Lyra shuddered. Her aunt had a truly awful story about what some of the worst fungi could do to a person, and she sincerely hoped that wasn't what they were dealing with.

Oddly, the thought of a necromancer turning bugbears into undead thralls, while horrible and extremely squicky, was somehow *less* disturbing than the alternative; a slime mold grabbing hold of a bunch of creatures and controlling them, for no other reason than that the slime mold reproduced by riding the nervous systems of living things until long past the point where they counted as living.

She wasn't sure why she felt more disturbed by the slime mold, though. Maybe because you could fight a necromancer? Defeat them? Get the problem to stop? But how did you fight a slime mold?

"You're right," Kiara said, clearly having observed Lyra's shudder. "The necromancer would be preferable."

Lyra chuckled nervously, now desperate to talk about something other than slime molds, and she reached for the first question that popped into her head.

"So… why didn't I see you at my aunt's funeral?" she asked. It was a question that had been nagging at her ever since they'd established that Kiara had not only known Aunt Vi, but had known her well enough to pick up some of her expressions and habits.

"Ah, that," Kiara sighed. "My team and I were out on assignment when Mage Stranglevine passed away. They told us the moment we got back, but we'd been gone for two months and we'd missed everything. Her death, the funeral, her Guild wake, all of it."

"Oh no! I'm so sorry. If I had known how close you two were, I would have asked them to delay part of it. We could have waited. When I asked the Guild if we should wait for anyone they just told me that everyone at the Guild who knew Aunt Vi would want to be there, but that if we waited for everyone who knew her to show up at the same time we'd never be able to hold the funeral, so…"

Kiara chuckled, and it didn't sound like it was full of resentment.

"They're right about that much. It's not the first time it's happened, and it won't be the last. Long assignments can be frustrating that way, but we usually get an extended leave after we return. My whole crew and I threw Mage Stranglevine a mini-wake of our own when we got the news."

That thought warmed a place in Lyra's chest that she was surprised to find needed warming.

"Oh good, she would have approved of an extra wake."

Kiara smiled then, and Lyra had to swallow the warmth that rose through her chest at the sight of the other woman's face alight with mischief.

"She would have, yes. As I imagine you know, Mage Stranglevine loved a good wake. And the Guild is particularly good at wakes. I suppose you could consider it a perk of the job if it didn't come from the increased risk of death and dismemberment."

Kiara's smile faded as she finished, but Lyra felt the corners of her own mouth tilting upwards as she thought of her aunt's oft-repeated refrain: "A person can die doing any damned thing on the planet; the fact that the Adventurer's Guild's members die doing something interesting, and preferably helpful, doesn't mean the job is any more risky than crossing a busy street on the way to work."

Lyra repeated the line while dipping her scone into the olive spread again and was surprised to find Kiara studying her intently when she finished.

"You can't believe that," the battle mage croaked.

Lyra frowned. Why did Kiara look so lost?

"I mean, sure I do. Aunt Vi said it often enough, and I looked up the statistics one time just to see if she was talking out of her ass, but it's true. The percentage of deaths from crossing at Main & Llweleth every year, as compared to the overall population of Dryvenvale, is higher than the percentage of deaths of Guild members dying on active duty compared to the population of the Guild."

"But... but... that can't be right."

"Why can't it be? You're not careless with your lives, are you?"

"No, of course not. I mean, no one who makes it past the first five years is, anyway. But we lose so many new recruits and—"

"Vi did say that the death rate for the Adventurer's Guild suffered a pretty extreme curve from year one to year five. But apparently, even with that factored in, it's still safer to be a Guild member than it is to cross a busy road in the middle of the day. I mean, statistically speaking. Not saying that throwing a bunch of untrained yahoos on a Guild adventure wouldn't result in more folks dying than crossing the road or anything, but that's not my understanding of how the Guild operates."

Lyra chuckled nervously while carefully watching Kiara's expression. The battle mage seemed to be going through something, but Lyra couldn't quite figure out what that might be.

Kiara shook her head before speaking.

"I can't decide if that means that we need to be shutting down the intersection at Main & Llweleth immediately, or if I need to find a more life-threatening form of occupation in order to keep up my reputation."

Lyra laughed loudly and almost sprayed a mouthful of olive spread across the room. Luckily, she clapped a hand over her mouth just in time.

"I mean, we definitely need to create a pedestrian over-pass over there, because really, no one should be dying just attempting to cross the street. But we also don't lose that many Guild members every year, do we? I mean, Vi usually only went to one or two wakes a year for her Guild buddies. And hells, at her age she went to twice that many funerals for her non-Guild friends."

Kiara blinked intently at the olive spread for a moment as she held another scone just above it, as though unsure if she should be dipping it in there. Lyra was fairly sure she wasn't puzzled by the olive spread itself, but she couldn't quite figure out what emotion was clouding Kiara's expression as she stared down at it. She hoped she hadn't just ruined the woman's self-image as a badass battle mage or anything. She didn't know what about the Adventurer's Guild had drawn Kiara to begin with, so she couldn't know if she'd just shattered something important about the woman's worldview or if something else was bothering her.

All she knew was that she wanted to do something to get that mischievous smile back on Kiara's face.

"... I MEAN..." Kiara couldn't get her mouth to work properly, and she wasn't certain her brain was working either, but she had to be sure of what the beautiful café owner had just told her, and for some reason it couldn't wait. She cleared her throat and tried again.

"So, *you* don't think that being in the Adventurer's Guild is too risky?"

Oh hells, now she knew why her brain had marked this as urgent. Kiara was flailing and falling fast. How could it be possible that Lyra didn't think being in the Guild was too dangerous? If Lyra didn't think that Kiara's job made her unlovable then Kiara had no reason to protect her heart, and if she had no reason to protect her heart then there was nothing to stop her from falling for the next café-owning goddess to slide down a vine in front of her after killing a zombie with a sewing machine.

Kiara swallowed and shook her head to dismiss that *oddly specific* example, but before she could distract herself Lyra was speaking again, and Kiara was hooked.

"Too risky for whom? Too risky for me? Maybe. I don't particularly enjoy having to fight for my life or anyone else's. Not enough that I'd want to do it every day anyway. But I didn't think it was too risky for Vi. It's clearly not too risky for *you*. You're eighteen years in and still going strong, right? It's fine for whoever wants to do it."

Ah, here it was. The lifeline that Kiara had been scrabbling for. It's fine for *other people* to do, but Kiara would bet her greatcoat that it wouldn't be fine for anyone Lyra cared about and who wasn't a parental figure. You couldn't exactly go around telling your caretaker her job was too risky, especially when she'd stopped doing that job the whole time you were too young to take care of yourself should anything have happened to her.

Feeling like salvation was at hand, Kiara pressed the point.

"But surely you wouldn't want someone you *loved*," Kiara swallowed—she *did not* need to be bandying that word about so casually, "like your child, for example, joining the Guild, right?"

Lyra turned her head to one side and looked at Kiara as if she'd just grown a second nose.

"Why would I stop my kid, or anyone else I loved, from doing a job they wanted to do?"

Kiara frowned, certain she couldn't be hearing this right.

"But you said…" She paused to remember what Lyra had said about when she'd been a child. "You said that Mage Stranglevine stopped working at the Guild when you were little. You said it like it was a good thing, and…

and you said you didn't want to be in the Guild yourself so... if you don't think it's too dangerous then why…" She had planned to fling all of Lyra's words back in her face, but now that she was trying to call them to mind she couldn't remember anything quite as damning as it had seemed at the time.

"You seriously can't think of any reasons I wouldn't want to join the Guild other than the danger?" Lyra asked, sounding truly perplexed.

"Well…" Kiara fumbled for something other than the refrain Evain had thrown at her whenever there had been tension in their relationship. *You can't expect me to just instantly be happy to see you after worrying for two months straight. I'm always prepared for you to not come back, so when you do, it's hard to adjust. How could you even think of wanting to bring a child into a world that likely won't have you in it as they grow up?* Kiara thought about sharing that quote with Lyra, but how could she? Wasn't it just the same argument she'd been making from the start?

Lyra laughed at the awkward pause, but it sounded more exasperated than amused.

"Look, I get it. You clearly enjoy being in the Guild, so maybe the drawbacks aren't as obvious to you but… Look, I grew up with stories of adventures and heroics and all of the legendary things that my aunt and her friends got up to when she was a young adventurer. I mean, they were my literal bedtime stories. But they didn't come from some storyteller in an inn trying to sway a crowd with tales of heroism; they came from the woman who had bled, sweated, and cried through every moment of those tales and… Aunt Vi never sugarcoated any of it."

Kiara snorted, finally distracted from her own anxious loop of thoughts because she could only imagine just how blunt Mage Stranglevine would have been as a parental figure.

Lyra's smile as she continued was nostalgic and loving, full of a fondness that called out to something inside Kiara as if from a very great distance.

"So from a very young age, it was clear to me that the whole adventuring thing was a mixed bag. Yes, sure, the feats of heroism, defending the innocent, fighting legendary monsters, clearing zombie-infested dungeons—it all sounded very impressive. But I also heard everything about the blisters, the forced marches, the sieges spent lying around waiting to die, or for food or allies to arrive first, the boredom, the grief, and… those bits never really appealed. But, when you get right down to it, the biggest part I wanted to avoid was… well, being gone from Dryvenvale for months at a time. I hated the idea of giving up all my hobbies, not seeing my friends, missing all the latest theatrical performances, missing out on dancing with my troupe… None of what the Guild was offering was worth missing out on all of those things in my mind. So why bother?"

"But your aunt giving up adventuring while you were a child, surely even SHE thought it was too dangerous if—"

"Kiara, she gave it up while I was a small child so that she wouldn't be GONE for months at a time. What kind of monster would leave a three-year-old who'd already lost both of her parents alone with strangers, or estranged family members so distant that they might as well be strangers, for the amount of time it takes to go on the average Guild assignment?"

Kiara swallowed and felt her cheeks warm with embarrassment.

"Right. Fair point. Well made."

But just because Lyra thought being a Guild battle mage was an acceptable profession didn't mean that she was open to dating one. Kiara couldn't for the life of her think of how to ask Lyra about it, though. At least not without implying that *Kiara* wanted some kind of romantic entanglement.

Did she want that? She had spent the past five years telling herself that she didn't. That she was perfectly happy alone. That if Kyle could be completely content without romance in his life, then why not her? But Est's voice rang in Kiara's memory.

You're not Kyle, Ki. Kyle has never had a romantic inclination in his entire life. YOU used to want to have a partner and start a family. We've discussed it at length more than once, on occasions when we've had a lot of time and a general sense that we might die soon. You wanted a partner and a family right up until that awful woman convinced you that you didn't deserve either, and I would like to light her on fire for that.

Considering that Est was one of the Guild's most respected healers, having her wish immolation on someone was rather extreme.

Kiara was just contemplating whether or not her interest in starting a family was relevant to their current discussion when Lyra changed the topic so dramatically that Kiara could barely follow what she said next.

"Where do you keep getting those playing cards?"

L YRA TRULY HADN'T meant to change the subject so abruptly, but as she'd been watching the elegant way the battle mage moved her neck and shoulders as she spoke, Lyra's gaze had eventually drifted down to her arms, sadly hidden by the thick leather greatcoat, and then the very fine hands of the grey-skinned half-elf. Then, for perhaps the hundredth time since they'd met, she had noticed Kiara pull a playing card from… somewhere… and begin tipping it through her long, elegant fingers.

"This?" Kiara asked, flicking the card forward so that Lyra could see the suit and number. It was an ace of hearts.

"Yes, I keep seeing them in your hand, but I've never been able to see where you get them."

Kiara smiled absently at the card and then leaned back against the nearest pile of gold. At a gesture from her, the left sleeve of her greatcoat lifted to her elbow, presumably as it had been spelled to do, then she used her hands to roll up the sleeve of her tunic. When she rotated her arm, Lyra could see a tattoo of an ace of hearts on the underside of her forearm. Then Kiara dropped both sleeves back in place and went back to flipping the card between her fingers.

"My grandfather always used to say that you should never go into battle without an ace up your sleeve. He was the one who taught me how to use my fire magic. He was also the only person in my family who didn't think I was wasting my time learning to become a battle mage. When he died, I got this tattoo in his memory, and then I couldn't resist getting it spelled to actually render playing cards. I just have to think of holding the card in my hand and it goes to my fingertips. The card itself is a token spell with two sides."

"A shield on one and a fireball on the other?" Lyra asked, even though she knew the answer.

"You noticed, huh?" Kiara smiled and ducked her head a bit.

"I'd have to be completely oblivious not to," Lyra murmured. "I assume you know some other spells. I mean, I think I saw a magic missile in there when you were fighting off some of the bugbears earlier, but if I hadn't been paying close attention, it would be easy to believe that a shield and a fireball were the only two spells in your book."

"Well, they were my go-tos even before I got this tattoo, but of course the tattoo makes it so that I don't have to use nearly as much energy to cast either shield or fireball; it's also much faster than a traditional casting, so, perfect for battle."

"Do you ever run out?" Lyra asked, curious now about how this particular tattoo had been spelled.

"I don't think the tattoo will ever stop manifesting the card when I want it, but I could use up all my own magic and then die horribly, same as anyone else, and the tattoo wouldn't stop that. If anything, it would just be one more thing to overdraw my magic on."

There was a long beat while they both took a moment to imagine the awful death that accompanied overdoing one's magic. Lyra was suddenly desperate to change topics again, so she blurted, "How long ago did your grandfather die?"

"About seven years ago now." Kiara's voice was quiet but didn't waver.

"I'm sorry you lost him." Lyra realized that this topic was still too close to the topic she'd hoped to avoid, but she refused to shift it again now. She wasn't so self-absorbed that she'd refuse to make space for someone else's grief just to avoid stepping in her own.

"Thanks," Kiara replied. "I am too. I always expected him to live forever. Or at least for a few more centuries.

He died fairly young for an elf, but… well, we can never predict who's going to go when, I suppose."

"Tell me about it. I honestly didn't think I was going to outlast Aunt Vi. I always expected that she'd keep going somehow, while the rest of us just lost our battles with time." *Great, Lyra, good job, you tried to create levity by asking about the playing cards, and then you steered yourself right into a conversation about grief, and when you tried to steer things away from mages dying of overtaxing their magic you steered right into the unfairness of dying early. Good job. Way to not make the conversation all about you and your trauma.* Lyra did not smack her own forehead, but only by exercising nearly superhuman restraint.

"I can see why you'd think that," Kiara agreed, clearly oblivious to Lyra's internal monologuing. "Mage Stranglevine seemed… inevitable. Like sunrise, or the tides."

Lyra laughed at that, because it was so very *true*. Then a stickier emotion caught in her throat as she thought of her aunt and just how... permanent she'd always seemed.

"It's just so incredibly unfair that she's gone, you know?"

Lyra braced herself as soon as the words fell out of her mouth. She hadn't meant to say them. She'd wanted to avoid this topic altogether, knowing that she would get "too emotional" if she started talking about her aunt again, knowing that she'd wind up killing the conversation entirely with how the loss of Violet had made her feel.

This was the part that a hardened warrior who'd been losing friends since she was a teenager was never going to understand. It was the part that neither Derva, who was no more a warrior than Lyra was herself, nor Rylan, who was every bit the battle mage that Kiara was, had ever been able to understand.

Lyra was *still* angry with the world for taking away one of the brightest parts of her life. And missing Aunt Vi still caught her like a physical blow sometimes, making her ache in all the places that were now hollow with her absence. The fact that no amount of time had been enough to heal the wound left in her heart had baffled first Rylan—the battle mage Lyra had been with when Aunt Violet had actually died—and then Derva—the completely non-magical dancer Lyra had taken up with after things fell apart with Rylan.

For all that Kiara seemed so much more understanding than either Rylan or Derva had been, Lyra was still certain that Kiara would be just as put off, if not more so. Kiara carried her grief so well; it clearly didn't rip her open the way Lyra's did. How could someone who held themselves together so competently in the face of their own sorrow possibly respect someone like Lyra, who might suddenly come apart at the seams even three years after the death of her aunt?

"It *is* incredibly unfair," agreed Kiara. "Hells, *I'm* still angry about it, and she was my mentor, not the woman who raised me."

Lyra's breath caught as those words sank into her, and she drew her eyes up from where she'd been watching the ace of hearts flip between the other woman's knuckles to look Kiara in the eyes. The half-elf's purple gaze was distant, but there was a frown on her lips as though she were remembering something unpleasant.

Lyra must have misunderstood.

"What do you mean?" she asked, even though she knew, she just... she couldn't fathom that Kiara agreed with her.

"It's stupidly unfair. Mage Stanglevine was fighting to protect an entire walled city from the kind of magical barrage that would have taken thousands of lives, and she was doing it because she decided long ago that defending the innocent was a job that was worth risking her own life. The fact that things got bad enough that she had to choose between her own life and that many civilian lives is ridiculous; the fact that reinforcements didn't arrive in time to spare her; the fact that no one else in her crew was adept enough to step in for her; the fact that the local government in that walled city let things get bad enough with a rogue group of cultists and their leader... there are a thousand things that should have happened differently to prevent Mage Stranglevine from ever having to make that choice, and it's absurd, cruel, unfair, and *wrong* that she was forced to choose between her own life and the lives of thousands."

Lyra felt tears streaming down her face as she listened to Kiara's words, though she could still just barely believe them. But the rough edge to Kiara's voice and the tears that streamed easily down the battle mage's own face made it clear just how much she meant what she was saying.

"The only thing that gives me any comfort," Kiara continued, "and it's cold comfort at that, is that *it worked*. Mage Stranglevine managed to make a strong enough barrier with that last bit of her magic that it protected the city long enough for reinforcements to arrive. But even knowing that the spell was stronger because she used up the last of herself with it, even knowing that it probably *wouldn't* have worked if she hadn't done that, and that she would have died along with everyone else when the cultists finally overwhelmed them... it doesn't make it hurt any less. It just... helps me to think that she would be proud of her work."

Lyra was outright sobbing now, even as she clung desperately to every word Kiara spoke.

Kiara had said nothing new—just given voice to words that Lyra had repeated in her mind a hundred times as she wrestled daily with the overwhelming sense of loss. But the idea that someone else understood the paradox of this particular grief, the deep knowledge that Aunt Vi would be *so glad* to know that her last-ditch effort to save all those peoples' lives had worked, that she would consider her own life a perfectly fair price to pay... knowing that *did* bring some small measure of peace to Lyra sometimes.

Just as often, though, the same knowledge infuriated her.

Hadn't Vi known that Lyra would be devastated by the loss? Hadn't she known that, no matter how many lives Vi had traded her own for, it could never make up for the hole in Lyra's heart? But Lyra knew the answers to those questions. She'd known them her whole life. Vi had actually explained it to her when she was very little.

"You know," Lyra croaked, when she could finally get her voice at least a little bit under her control, "for all that she went on about the death rates of Guild members not being higher than crossing the road, she always knew she'd likely die protecting someone. She predicted her own death, and gods, she even told me..."

Lyra chuckled soggily to herself, wiping at her nose and eyes with her sleeve before continuing. Kiara's eyes were focused directly on hers; but she couldn't bear to hold the other woman's gaze while she got this out, so she just stared into the middle distance of the golden glow inside the cursed chest and let the words pour out of her.

"When she first went back to adventuring, when I was finally apprenticed and living on my own... I asked her why she wanted to go back and she told me all the reasons that she loved her job and... well, by then I was old enough that I was suddenly horrified at the idea that *I* had been the reason she'd stopped doing something she loved."

Lyra shook her head at the memory. She'd been so upset at the mere idea that she might have kept Vi from something she loved that the moment the idea had occurred to her she had run into Vi's room, interrupting her in the middle of cleaning her gear, and dropped to her knees with tears running down her face.

"I asked her if she resented me for keeping her from adventuring for so many years, but she told me she hadn't even considered it an option. When I'd been handed over to her and she'd become my guardian, she'd known instantly that she could never do her job while I was young enough to need her, because she'd never be able to leave me for that long when she was the only thing I had left. She also said she'd never have been able to sacrifice herself to save others when doing so would leave me alone in the world, so there was no point in her returning to the Guild when she would refuse to do her job properly."

Lyra sighed, remembering the fire in Vi's eyes when she'd nearly shouted at Lyra that she wouldn't allow her to feel a shred of guilt for what had been a choice Vi had made without even a single moment of regret. Aunt Vi had reassured her, in no uncertain terms, that she hadn't even missed her adventuring days while Lyra was growing up, because every day with Lyra was an adventure of its own.

"Once she saw I had people, that I had friends, lovers, a community of good people in my life that would be with me through everything…that was when she knew she could go back to work, because she knew if someone needed her to give up her life to save them, she could. She could do it knowing that I would understand what she'd had to do, and that I would know it didn't mean she loved me any less. She just… believed I had enough love in my life to fill in the gaps."

Lyra was still sobbing. She was just squeezing the words out between gasps.

It hurt *so much* to say those words out loud, but it hurt worse to keep them trapped inside, so she let them come anyway.

"And I *do* understand," she continued, doggedly, "And I *don't* hate her for the choice she made. She was just being herself. Her true self. There was no version of the Vi I loved who could have let those people die to save her own life. That was part of why I loved her so damned much. But I am absolutely furious with the world for forcing that choice on her, and I don't think anyone else understands why I'm so damned angry about it."

Lyra could barely see through her tears, but despite being a sobbing, snotty mess she could feel Kiara shift beside her, and there was no way to avoid hearing the soft "Can I hug you?" from the mage.

Lyra couldn't get her voice to work again, so she simply nodded, and immediately felt Kiara's arms wrap around her.

Lyra marveled for a moment at how comfortable, and comforting, the other woman's embrace was. Maybe it was the strong leather scent of the greatcoat mixed with fire magic that reminded her of Aunt Vi, or maybe the strength in Kiara's arms just radiated support, but somehow it didn't feel like being hugged by a stranger.

Of course, that only served to redouble the sobs that had taken hold of Lyra's chest. Gods, when was the last time that Lyra had felt comforted?

And then she laughed at herself.

She'd been comforted by any number of her friends since Aunt Vi had died. Her friends loved her, and they loved her no matter how broken she'd felt by her aunt's death. They were all as generous in their love as they were in their acceptance of what the loss of Aunt Vi had done to her.

They never expected her to be fine when she was not fine.

Her friends were good people and they understood that she was not "over" her aunt's death, and never would be. Then she almost rolled her eyes at herself as she recalled that it was, in fact, only her friends' unconditional acceptance of her, no matter how broken she felt or how broken she behaved, that had led her to finally understanding that Derva had not been good for her, and that neither had Rylan.

Eventually, Lyra had realized that if *her friends* could make allowances for how broken she still was after losing Aunt Violet, then Derva should have been able to do the same.

But...

"This is where my ex would have told me that I was being selfish," she mumbled into Kiara's shoulder. She was vaguely aware that she was leaving quite a few tears and no small amount of snot on the battle mage's greatcoat, but she figured it probably wasn't more than the spellwork that had repelled light spinner ichor and zombie bugbear guts could handle, so she promptly stopped worrying about it.

"I'm gonna need you to explain that one," Kiara said in a quiet voice above her. "Well, I mean, I'm not sure anyone can explain that one, but please tell me what that person thought they meant because..."

Lyra sighed and considered whether or not she could surreptitiously rub the tears from her eyes and wipe her nose using her sleeve. But she really didn't want to move away from this hug, so instead she cast a quickdry spell on her face.

Somehow, talking of Derva made it easy to forget the pain of losing Aunt Vi for a moment.

"Well, my ex was emphatic that grief was only for the living. Which is true enough, but… she also thought that I was being ungrateful for what I had every time I let my sadness over losing Vi 'distract' me from my day-to-day life."

Kiara had leaned back a bit, in order to look Lyra in the eyes, and now she kept her gaze steady on Lyra's as she said, clearly and distinctly, "Well, that's utter horseshit."

Lyra was so surprised she laughed.

"Well, it took you a lot less time to realize that than it took me. I let her make me feel guilty for mourning Aunt Vi for a good year and a half before I realized she was the only person who claimed to love me and also told me I was being unreasonable for being sad about Vi still."

Kiara took a deep breath and let it out slowly before she replied, "Please don't ever introduce me to this woman. I will probably set her shoes on fire."

Lyra chuckled again, and then took a moment to register that Kiara still hadn't let go of her. She found that she didn't particularly mind.

"I have no reason to introduce you to her, as I don't see her anymore. We did not part on very good terms, I'm afraid. But I'm embarrassed to admit that it took me a *lot* longer to get rid of the hold her words had on me than it did to get rid of her. I spent a long time telling myself I just needed to get over it… but eventually I realized that wasn't actually a thing. Or at least, not a healthy thing."

"I'm afraid not," agreed Kiara. "I suppose maybe there's someone out there for whom grief heals like a wounded leg—getting better and better until someday it's as good as it was before and all that's left is a scar, but… well, that hasn't been my experience at all, nor has it been the experience of any of my close friends or family. For me, grief has always been a wound that you carry for life. It gets a bit less raw around the edges perhaps, or maybe even scabs over, but it's always there, and the best you can do is learn not to poke at it too hard."

Lyra nodded. "Yeah, I think of Aunt Vi every single day, and it always hurts when I remember she's not here… Most days it doesn't hurt as much as it did when I first found out… but… some days it does."

"Sounds about right," Kiara agreed, her voice soft. Lyra *felt* the words more than she heard them, since she was pressed against Kiara's chest, her head on the half-elf's shoulder, and Kiara's mouth seemed to be pressed into her hair.

After a long moment of silence in which neither of them seemed inclined to move, Lyra finally said, "Well, this is nice."

Kiara laughed, and the motion shook them both. Lyra enjoyed the sound almost as much as she enjoyed the feel of Kiara's body moving against her.

"You have a thing for getting trapped inside cursed chests with women you've just met?" Kiara asked, and her voice had shifted slightly, in a way that made Lyra's skin tingle with expectation.

Lyra chuckled in return. She wanted to look into the battle mage's purple eyes again, but she didn't want to risk breaking the hug.

"No," she admitted, "but being comfortable in someone else's arms is no small thing, even if one is trapped inside of a cursed chest and expecting to die of eventual starvation."

"I thought we'd established we had enough food and water that we probably wouldn't starve or dehydrate?" Kiara said.

"Oh right. I'd almost forgotten."

"Really?"

"No, but it sounded much more dramatic, don't you think?"

"Can't argue with that."

"So... I suppose we should start looking for a way out of here, shouldn't we?"

"Yes. We probably should."

Neither of them moved.

"But maybe in a few more minutes?" Kiara offered, her voice gentle.

Lyra simply nodded and continued to lean against Kiara's shoulder, while the other woman ran her fingers slowly up and down Lyra's spine.

Chapter Nine
Astral Physics

K IARA WAS STARING at the top of Lyra's beautiful, emerald green hair, her nose full of the scent of coffee, pastries, and a hint of lemon, while considering how inappropriate it would be to kiss a woman who had just spent the past five minutes crying on her shoulder.

She desperately wanted to, and she had a suspicion that Lyra would be open to the idea, but she also knew that the woman was probably feeling particularly vulnerable after everything she'd just shared, and Kiara did not like thinking she might be taking advantage of her vulnerability.

She rather desperately wanted Lyra to want her, but *not* because she was the only comforting body in a pocket dimension.

"Lyra?" Kiara asked, trying to keep her voice steady and calm even as the other woman was pressed so close that she could feel the curves of her body through the thick leather of her greatcoat.

"Mmmm?" Lyra's voice sounded hazy and... surely Kiara was imagining the lust she thought she heard there?

Kiara swallowed. It was patently unfair for someone to make that kind of noise in their throat when you could feel it against your chest... and all the way down to your bones.

This purple-skinned, green-haired goddess who descended from vines using nothing but her legs, who always carried cheese and olive spread, and who could kill a zombie with nothing but an ancient sewing machine and some creative problem-solving, had been slowly tearing down the wall that Kiara had so carefully constructed around her heart in the years since Evain had left her, and now... now Kiara'd had a terrible idea that she couldn't seem to let go of.

"I would very much like to take you on a *real* date when we get out of here. Somewhere... oh, I don't know... less populated with zombies. Perhaps even a bit less cursed, in general?"

Lyra shifted against Kiara until their eyes met, and between the feel of Lyra's body as she moved, and the look in Lyra's eyes when their gazes locked, Kiara had to swallow *again* to keep herself from leaning down and claiming the other woman's mouth with her own.

"That sounds lovely," Lyra said, smiling so warmly that Kiara wondered if she'd accidentally set herself on fire underneath her greatcoat. "Not that this hasn't been fun in its own way, but... yes, I think a date with fewer zombies would be an excellent choice."

Kiara couldn't stop herself from laughing at the tone Lyra's voice took on the word 'fun', as if she'd never used a word less sincerely in her entire life.

"Excellent!" Kiara said, with no small relief. Her fingers practically tingled with it. "Then consider it a date! Now we just have to get out of here."

"Hmmm... I suppose we should. Gwen is probably getting worried and—" Lyra abruptly sat up, pulling far enough away from Kiara that she wanted to reach out and claw the woman back to her, but only after she set fire to whatever it was that made Lyra look so worried.

"Oh, Og's Balls, Gwen's pendant! I saw it when we first fell in here and I meant to grab it, but then we were trying to sort out how much food we had, and then we were getting all maudlin about the people we've lost and then there was the cuddling and… I forgot."

Lyra stood up, her eyes already frantically sweeping the area around them, and Kiara was instantly cold in all the places where their bodies had been pressed against one another. Not knowing what else to do, she stood up as well, wondering if she had all the components for a seek spell on her if Lyra couldn't find the pendant in all of this treasure.

But Lyra only looked around the space for another moment, her emerald eyes scanning the piles of gold and silver with keen interest, before she took a few steps towards one of the piles and then bent over to pick something up.

Kiara was opening her mouth to ask if she'd found Gwen's pendant when Lyra simply vanished.

L YRA HAD NO idea what in the seven hells was going on, but she was getting very tired of surprises. She had felt herself get sucked through space and time—in the uncomfortable way that portals took a person from one place to the next—the instant she'd grabbed hold of Gwen's pendant, so she'd been expecting to find herself somewhere new. She really had *not* expected the new place to be her own broom cupboard, but that had to be where she was. It still smelled like all the coffee, tea and sanitary products that had been stored there before they'd moved it all out for Auryl to take over.

She blinked as her eyes adjusted to the dim glow of the fairy lights and the mirror portal, then found the tiny dragon looking up quizzically at her from a nearby shelf.

"Why am I here?" she asked, before Auryl could even open their mouth to speak.

"I do not know," replied the dragon. "This does not happen."

For a moment Lyra was so confused about where she was—or, more accurately, where she *wasn't*—that she didn't even remember that she was furious with the little dragon for dropping her into a cursed forest.

"What do you mean, *this does not happen?*"

Auryl blinked at her for a moment and then said, "You did not follow the trail to the exit portal with your companion. There is no other way out of the dungeon. This should not be possible."

"The dungeon?" Lyra asked, getting more confused by the second. "You mean the forest?"

"Forest, dungeon, it's all the same. It is a confined space full of mortal peril, even if it is not surrounded by stone walls and iron gates."

Lyra shook her head, trying to get her brain to catch up to her body. Her body seemed to be shaking with rage, but she wasn't entirely sure why yet, so she stuck to the immediate. "I don't care about the semantics! WHY AM

I HERE? Where is Kiara? WHAT DID YOU DO TO HER?!?"

Ah yes, there we go. Lyra was feeling as though something had been stolen, either an opportunity, or perhaps just a person. Either way, her fingers were getting ready to call water to her whim, and she was willfully not thinking about how quickly a dragon, even a pocket-sized dragon, could squash her with its magic.

"I did nothing to her," the pocket-sized dragon in question said, its tone calm. "I have not done anything to either of you. You both agreed to the terms of the spell, and you were doing just fine until that... that... thing swallowed you. I have been unable to see what was happening ever since that creature ingested you. I did not think any harm had come to you because the spell would not allow that, but... I do not like being unable to see my clients."

"What do you mean, the spell would not allow us to be harmed? What happened to your whole last-second word-spew of special conditions right before we stepped through the portal? What happened to SURVIVAL NOT GUARANTEED?!?"

Lyra was beginning to remember all her earlier anger now; it piled happily on top of the anger that had started when she'd realized she'd been ripped away from Kiara. She ignored the small voice inside her saying that half of that rage was actually fear. She determinedly did *not* think about what could happen to Kiara if she was still trapped in that cursed chest when the bugbears caught up to it.

Auryl seemed oblivious to her rage, or else had no reason to react to it. Their voice was still smooth and a tiny bit condescending—in other words, draconic—as they said, "If you do not think anything bad can happen to you, you are less likely to treat all the monsters and other threats seriously. But if you do not take the threats seriously, you will not bond properly over your time spent evading and defeating them. I do not understand *why* two-legged people behave so oddly, but it has been proven many times that mortal threats cement bonds that other activities do not."

"So you made us think we could actually die so that we'd... what, bond more quickly?"

"More or less."

Lyra felt a different rage boil up inside her—this one tinged with the embarrassment that always accompanied being swindled.

"Gods, do you even *try* to find people who are actually compatible, or do you just throw together anyone at all and let the adrenaline do all the work?"

Now the little dragon looked offended, sitting back on their tiny haunches with a brief burst of smoke coming from their little nostrils. Lyra hated that she still found it adorable, even while it was condescendingly explaining things to her.

"My magic is excellent at selecting people who are likely to form long-term relationships. I take my work *very* seriously. I would never put two people into the same spell whom I did not think would make a suitable long-term match. My quality assurance standards are quite high, and I take great pride in how many people have fallen in love through my services. Do you not think that you and your battle mage would make a good match, even if you had simply met on the street someday?"

Lyra didn't want to think about that question, because she was starting to wonder if Kiara would have been half as understanding about Lyra's grief if they hadn't been thrown together into dire circumstances. Hadn't the woman been standoffish for the whole first part of the date? Lyra had written off Kiara's early brusk demeanor as a normal reaction to finding oneself dropped into a cursed forest with zero warning, but what if the woman had just been completely uninterested in Lyra until the adrenaline had kicked in and their emotions had been running high?

Would Kiara regret asking Lyra on a second date the moment she set foot back in Dryvenvale?

Lyra shook those questions away; they didn't matter right now.

She wasn't sure if she was reassured knowing that Auryl thought she and Kiara would make a good couple. She wasn't even sure she trusted the little dragon, and she still felt a bit like she'd been swindled. After all, she only had Auryl's word that the cursed forest couldn't *actually* hurt them, and maybe that was why she still felt like this whole thing was a mess.

She took a deep breath and let it out slowly, hoping to calm the maelstrom of emotions that swept through her so she could focus on the problems that part of her brain insisted were more urgent. Things did not add up yet.

"So, if no one can get hurt in your cursed forest, then why did it feel like those zombified bugbears were trying to kill us?"

"Oh, they were. And it is *not* my cursed forest. It is simply *a* cursed forest. *My spell* is what would protect you from those bugbears in their unfortunate state. They were truly attempting to kill you, presumably by order of their master, but had you been unsuccessful at defending against them, my spell would have warded you from their attacks."

Now the little dragon sounded full of pride as it continued. "It works best when it has something to help it along, though, so every fight you were in was... let us say *boosted* by my spell."

"Is that why the light spinners didn't manage to bite me that whole time?"

"You did an admirable job of evading them! It is possible that they might have managed to sink their mandibles into you without the help of my spell, but I cannot be certain that you wouldn't have kept them off all on your own. They are not very creative combatants, as you witnessed. They truly expect their food to stumble into their trap and then lie quiet while they are devoured."

Lyra realized she was getting distracted by the particulars and shook her head again.

"We need to have this conversation later, certainly before I let you put any of my customers through anything like this, but definitely *after* we get Kiara out of there! Kiara is in that cursed chest all alone, and that means she's trapped in there until I go back and get her, isn't she?"

Auryl mumbled quietly for a moment, "The vine creature is a cursed chest? Hmmm... that explains... but no. It can't be... That is," the tiny dragon cleared their throat, and then continued in a louder, more confident voice, "possibly. The cursed chest was a surprise. My spell *should* protect her from all harm in the cursed forest... but as the inside of any cursed chest is a pocket dimension, technically, it is no longer part of the cursed forest."

"Well, you have to send me back then!"

"I cannot. I have no connection to the inside of the cursed chest. It is, as I have mentioned, a separate dimension."

"Then send me to the outside of the cursed chest and I'll do the rest, but damn it all, we can't just leave her there!"

Lyra wasn't sure why she was so determined to go back to that stupid cursed forest to save, of all people, a battle mage who could obviously take care of herself, but she had felt ever so slightly out of place ever since she'd been pulled away from Kiara without warning. She needed to get back to her. Auryl frowned, staring at the portal. When Lyra turned to look at it over her shoulder, it was a swirl of bright lights, but didn't seem to be showing anything useful. Like, for example, the location of the cursed chest.

"I still do not understand how you are here," Auryl muttered, sounding vexed. "It should not be possible to exit the cursed chest on your own, let alone to bypass the remainder of the forest trail and…" their voice trailed off.

Lyra was *not* reassured.

"I was just as stuck in there as you'd expect, although we hadn't really gotten around to trying to find a way out yet, but I went to pick up Gwen's pendant and—Oh shit! Where is Gwen?"

Lyra looked down and saw that her fingers were still curled around the shining mithril of Gwen's pendant, but she couldn't feel the panther's consciousness on the other end.

"Who is Gwen?" asked Auryl.

Lyra blinked at the tiny dragon for a moment, before replying somewhat incredulously, "The enormous ethereal panther that was with us? Surely, if you've been keeping an eye on us, you've seen her? She's a nine-hundred-pound purple cat; she's kind of impossible to miss."

"Ah, yes, I had assumed she was the battle mage's familiar."

Lyra rolled her eyes. She didn't care if the tiny dragon could snap her like a twig, magically speaking. She was done. "No, she's *my* familiar. Or rather, she's her own cat, but since she can't be here without an oath to someone from this realm, we've sworn for each other."

Auryl blinked their oversized eyes at her and Lyra sighed, expecting to have to yet again explain how she was able to control a powerful ethereal panther when she was "just a hearth witch," but this time, Auryl surprised her.

"Not very many mages in this realm are considerate enough to swear their own oaths to their ethereal companions."

"Yeah, well, it's a shitty tradition if you ask me. The only reason that the ethereals don't seem to mind is that they're very curious about our realm and tend to outlive us by millennia, so I guess it works out for them. My Aunt Vi always said it was a bum deal, so she struck a different bargain with her familiar. When Aunt Vi passed, I couldn't stand the thought of losing Gwen, too, but it turned out Gwen didn't want to leave me either, so that made the whole thing pretty simple. We made our own vows, and they're enough to keep the mage council appeased, but we may have glossed over some of the finer details of what we swore."

Lyra didn't know why she was telling Auryl all of that. It wasn't as though she trusted the tiny dragon in particular. But the way Auryl had said 'not very many mages' had made her want to explain that she wasn't as mule-headed as 'many mages' were.

Auryl nodded in response, and Lyra thought it was a respectful motion, but she reminded herself that they didn't really have time to justify all of her actions to the little dragon.

"So, Kiara. How do I get back to her?"

"Well, I believe that I now understand *how* you got here. If that pendant connects to your familiar and they are from the ethereal plane, then… likely when you touched the pendant inside of the chest, if your familiar was

146

attempting to reach you at the same time, it would have caused... well, I cannot seem to translate the concept from Draconic to Common... too many portals? Too many dimensions? Hmmm… we have a perfectly good word for this, but it appears that your realm's languages do not share the term."

The tiny dragon looked truly annoyed by the lack of vocabulary, but seemed determined to explain. "Look, the ethereal plane cannot be contained within a pocket dimension, yes? An object that connects to the ethereal plane might be *stored* in a pocket dimension, but if anyone were to attempt to use that item, it would have to be ejected from the pocket dimension in order to allow it to function. But, then, if ejecting you from the cursed chest would have put you in harm's way within the cursed forest, then *my* spell *might* have intervened and ejected you here instead. But that means—"

And now the tiny voice that had been ringing in Lyra's mind since she'd arrived here, the one that had made her start asking about Kiara right away instead of all the other questions that she'd been meaning to ask the tiny dragon, that voice was now screaming.

"That means that the cursed chest is in mortal peril," Lyra breathed. "Kiara. Gwen! You have to get me back to them RIGHT NOW!"

She wanted to grab the creature to make it comply, but that would either have been cruel or unfathomably stupid, depending on whether or not it was as physically fragile as it was magically overpowered.

Auryl looked suddenly pale, which was not a thing that Lyra had thought dragons could do. Not that she knew much at all about dragon anatomy. Maybe they flushed and paled just like she did. Regardless, she didn't take it as a good sign.

"I will try," Auryl assured her. "But—"

"No buts, Auryl! We can't just leave them in there. Gwen can survive just about anything, but she feels pain just like anyone else, and I don't want her getting ripped to pieces by some zombified bugbear! And Kiara... it's not like she needs my help in a fight, but if she's trapped inside of that cursed chest, then there's nothing she can do to save herself! You have to get me back there so I can get her out!"

"The spell will not allow me to return you to mortal peril!"

Lyra felt a brief stab of fear low in her gut, the kind that she felt standing at the top of a trapeze just before flying. The kind that told her she might die if she did the next thing she was planning to do. But just like she did when she was about to perform, she shook that fear away. Gwen needed her, and, gods damn her for caring so much already, but Kiara needed her too.

"Then send me back without the damned spell."

"Lyra, no! If I send you back without the spell, you'll be unprotected! The bugbears could kill you! You could fall off a cliff! Or a rock could hit you in the head! ANYTHING could happen! And people are so stupidly fragile."

Lyra took a deep breath. She'd known all of that the moment she'd suggested it, but it didn't matter.

"Auryl, the whole time we've been in there I thought we could die. Hells, I was so certain that we *were* going to die that I honestly thought you were trying to kill us. It may not have been true then, but I believed it was, and this won't be any different. I already thought everything was on the line. Now I'll just be right about it. But that doesn't change anything. I can't just leave them there. I won't call

Gwen back to the pendant if she's still trying to protect Kiara, because she'd be furious with me if I did. And I won't abandon Kiara to whatever the hells is going on in there. All I have to do is get her out of the chest and then she and Gwen can battle their way out, and I'll just stay out of the way. You said we were doing pretty well on our own, right? How many times did the spell have to protect us?"

Auryl stared blankly at her for a few moments before nodding—though they still looked pale, and honestly a bit lost. "Not that many. You... you have decent odds of surviving... or at least... well, better than 50% by my calculations."

Lyra felt a humorless laugh escape her.

"I guess I'll take it."

"Lyra, this is…" Now the little dragon looked truly somber for the first time since they'd started speaking, and Lyra couldn't help but want to comfort it somehow. "I'm so sorry. This was never meant to be truly dangerous. This kind of thing has never happened before... I... I'm sorry."

Lyra couldn't help but notice that the tiny dragon's voice was deeper now than it had been before, and that ever since she'd arrived in the cupboard the dragon's syntax and manner of speaking had been far more clear-cut and fluent in Common than they had sounded earlier.

She wasn't exactly surprised to discover that the little dragon leaned into being small, cute, and easily underestimated. She knew plenty of people who played similar tricks against a world that was all too happy to make assumptions about people based on appearances, but... she made a mental note that she would need to have a very serious discussion with Auryl when this was over. If the little dragon wanted to run a business inside of her café, they really needed to talk about expectations, honesty, and what she was willing to allow her customers to believe.

Assuming she survived this rescue operation.

"Ok," she said, shaking out her wrists and taking a few deep breaths to level her head. "Can you show me where I'm going before I go through?"

Auryl frowned, staring hard at the portal for a moment, as though perhaps trying to adjust its settings. Lyra didn't create many portals herself—just the basic ones she used for storage, not the kind that could cover huge distances and still be aimed to a new location without interrupting the spell—so she could only guess at what the dragon was actually doing.

"The spell doesn't know where Kiara is, because she's technically no longer in the cursed forest. And it doesn't recognize ethereals, so I can't even use your familiar as a locus. It also doesn't recognize the cursed chest as a living thing, even though it seems to be sentient, so I cannot use that either. So... the best I can do is put you back where you were just before the chest swallowed you. But I can already see the chest is no longer there. You are heading to an empty bit of forest, and that's the best I can do."

Lyra sighed. She hadn't really expected better, but she'd certainly hoped for it.

"It doesn't matter," she said, as much to herself as to Auryl. "I'll find them. That damned chest is constantly shrieking like the unrestful dead, and I can climb a tree to scout ahead if I need to."

She hoped it was true.

She hoped she wasn't about to go get clubbed to death by a bugbear. She had no particular interest in dying anytime soon, but she would be damned to the nine hells if she was going to let her... date? Friend? Potential future lover? Ach! Labels be damned, she wasn't going to let *Kiara* die trapped inside a box.

So she nodded once, flicked out her wrists one last time, and stepped into the portal.

HE STEPPED OUT in a very dark, mostly empty bit of forest on the other side of the portal, and honestly felt a bit disappointed. Not that she'd *wanted* to stumble directly into a zombified bugbear trying to kill her, but after everything else arriving in a bit of forest where not even the cursed vines were trying to grab her just felt a bit anticlimactic.

Then she heard the cursed chest shriek, and she forgot all about dramatic expectations and started running.

It was much harder going than it had been when Kiara had been burning a swath through the underbrush. Lyra was following a path cut by the cursed chest back when she'd still thought of it as the "vine creature" which meant that the underbrush, young trees, dangling vines, and more plant species than Lyra had ever learned to name, had been cut low by the sheer momentum of the giant chest and its many writhing vine legs. But even still, in the trail that was left behind there were roots covered in moss thick on the ground, and vines that hung down from beyond where the vine creature's bulk had cleared things, which seemed all too happy to grab for her as she walked beneath them. She remembered all the vines that she'd been on guard for since the moment they'd entered this forest, and she tried not to think that the only thing that had kept them from strangling her might have been the protection spell that Auryl had placed on them.

"Dag's tits, if I die on this date, I'm going to haunt that little dragon to the ends of the earth and back."

Lyra? called a voice so familiar that Lyra nearly wept with relief.

Gwen! Where are you?

Follow the shrieking. I'm trying to keep the vine-covered chest protected. How did you escape?

I'm not entirely sure, but according to the little dragon your pendant was in the chest and when I touched it, the universe balked and spat me out of Auryl's portal.

Interesting.

You sound distracted, Gwen.

I'm fighting a half-dozen bugbear zombies.

Right. I'll leave you to it. On my way!

Lyra had a million more questions, but none that were worth distracting Gwen when she was in the middle of fighting that many zombic bugbears away from the chest that currently had Kiara trapped inside it.

Fortunately, between the chest's earsplitting shrieks, and the swath of forest cutting a trail as wide as Lyra was tall, it wasn't difficult to decide where to go. It also helped that Gwen was near the chest, and now that Lyra was back in the same general location as the panther, she had a strong sense of where her familiar was. She had looped Gwen's pendant over her neck as she'd been stepping into the portal, and now she was holding it tight to keep it from hitting her in the face as she ran.

Lyra heard the chest let out another shriek and then, as her feet carried her down a steep slope and she had to jump over a series of enormous fallen logs coated in thick green moss soaked with some past rain, she could suddenly hear the sounds of claws rending flesh, bugbears groaning in zombified displeasure, and the occasional hiss of a very large, very angry feline.

All of which meant that she was getting close enough that it was time to find a solid vine to climb. Lyra might have made the decision to execute this rash excuse for a one-woman rescue mission, but she held no illusions about her chances of surviving a direct attack on half a dozen bugbears. She needed to get some perspective and make a plan.

KIARA WAS SURROUNDED by molten puddles of gold. The smell was odd: a combination of heat and metal that reminded her a little of the Guild's forge, but with the added buzz of unharnessed magic. She should probably be worried about that bit—destroying a bunch of unknown magical items in close proximity was not the smartest plan, especially in a contained space—but she was too angry to stop.

It wasn't that she thought melting the entire horde of gold stored within the cursed chest would help, exactly, but she lacked other targets and she'd already eaten all the cheese that Lyra had left behind when she disappeared.

Kiara couldn't for the life of her figure out where Lyra had gone, or how she'd managed to leave.

She was fairly certain that the woman hadn't *meant* to leave. That much had been clear enough from the brief expression of shock on Lyra's face just as she'd winked out of existence.

Also, Kiara would bet her greatcoat that Lyra wouldn't have tried to leave this place without her, despite only having known her for a handful of hours. After all, the café owner had taken on a dozen light spinners just to make sure Kiara didn't get left behind and consumed. She didn't think that leaving Kiara to starve inside of a cursed chest was on Lyra's list of to-dos.

"Ugh. I really have too much faith in a woman I just met. It's entirely possible she and that damned dragon rigged this entire thing as a very elaborate trap and…" Kiara sighed, melting yet another pile of coins into puddledom. It did *not* actually seem entirely possible. She couldn't even imagine Lyra plotting like that. Or, rather, she could absolutely imagine Lyra outsmarting her enemies in some extremely clever and elaborate way, but… she couldn't really imagine Lyra considering her an enemy. Not after the conversations they'd had in here. Not after the cheese, scones and olive spread.

"I was fairly certain she wanted to kiss me earlier," she murmured to no one in particular. Not that enemies don't ever kiss, if Est's favorite romance novels were to be believed, but… well, it was probably stupid, and hopefully it wouldn't get her killed, but her gut absolutely refused to believe that Lyra was the enemy. Her gut had never yet gotten her killed, so she was going to go with it. Which meant that Lyra had been removed from this cursed treasure hole, and now Kiara had no way to get to her, and she could be stuck fighting zombified bugbears right now and Kiara wouldn't be there to help.

Three more piles of gold were reduced to molten puddles, and Kiara wiped sweat from her brow onto the stiff leather sleeve of her greatcoat.

"It's going to get unbearably warm in here if I keep this up much longer…" she muttered—which, strangely, gave her an idea.

Chapter Ten
Inspiration

YRA WAS PROBABLY about to die, but she didn't really see any other options.

She was, once again, hanging upside down from a branch she'd reached by climbing a vine she'd had to subdue first (since it had been trying rather obviously to wrap itself around her neck). The scene below her was mayhem, and the smell of crushed bugbear zombie, mixed with the sounds of claws tearing into undead flesh, wasn't helping the nausea she sometimes experienced when she stayed upside down for too long.

She absolutely did not *want* to die, and she was going to try like hell not to, but there were only so many times that a person could drop an iron sewing machine on top of bugbear zombies before they caught on to your tricks.

Granted, that was already many more times than she'd dared hope for—she'd squished two of them without getting anywhere near Gwen, and was already lining up her aim on a third—but sooner or later they were going to notice their dwindling numbers and shift their focus away from the chest that Gwen was doing her damnedest to protect. Then Lyra would be in serious trouble.

"What in the seven hells do they even want the cursed chest for? They're DEAD already. It's full of random bits of gold. What do zombies even want with gold?"

Lyra knew that shouting was not a good idea. She didn't need to draw more attention from the undead bugbears than she'd already managed with her repeated sewing machine trick, but she figured Gwen could use a break by now. There were four bugbears on the ground, in too many pieces to constitute a threat even if those pieces kept twitching, but that still left far too many up and about trying to kill her only remaining family.

Ah, well, the shouting must have finally done it. Adjusting the aim on her bag of holding, she felt the branch that she was clinging to with only her legs *sway.* And not in the way that a branch might sway in the wind, or because she'd shifted her weight on it. No, it was definitely swaying to the force of the bugbear zombie who had finally cottoned on to her tricks and had its arms wrapped around the base of the tree that held her nice, comfortable branch.

This made it quite a bit harder for her to aim her final sewing machine strike, but she figured it was worth it if that meant there was one less bugbear zombie swinging its club at Gwen.

Of course, the next time she looked at the bugbear shaking her tree in an effort to time her next shot so that the shaking caused the least interference possible, she realized *that* bugbear was the least of her concerns.

Sure, the shaking was obnoxious and her branch was swaying more than she would have liked, but it was still holding, and she had spent far too long hanging upside down and spinning herself on purpose for performances to be thrown off by a bit of swaying.

No, the problem was definitely the smaller zombie bugbear—and where had that one even come from? Had the bugbears sent for reinforcements? She could have sworn this smaller one hadn't been there when she'd first arrived—that had climbed right over top of the one shaking the tree, and was now slowly—thank all the gods it wasn't fast, the world did not need fast zombies—grappling its way up the trunk. She had to assume it was headed for her branch.

The smaller zombie wasn't very nimble. It seemed heavy, and it moved like whoever was driving had never once in their life been an actual bugbear. Nevertheless, Lyra had to admit that eventually it was going to reach her branch, and then she was going to die horribly.

Because the moment the bugbear tried to crawl out on her branch—even a small bugbear weighed quite a bit more than Lyra herself did—the branch was going to snap, and then she was either going to plummet over thirty feet onto the forest floor, or plummet over thirty feet onto a zombie bugbear, and either way she didn't think she would get up and walk away from that.

She was more than a little frustrated that the zombie bugbears had developed a sudden capacity to take actions beyond swinging enormous clubs, but she supposed it was too much to hope that they would remain oblivious to the repeated threat of sewing machines squashing their comrades.

A niggling voice in her mind suggested that the bug-bears were more versatile because Auryl's spell was no longer protecting them, but she told that voice to shut the hells up—not because it was wrong, but because it wasn't helpful.

Lyra sighed; she needed to find a new strategy anyway. Her Great Gram's Slinger 300 had been a surprisingly effective zombie crusher, but it was now fractured in enough places that Lyra despaired of even her favorite dwarven smith being able to fix it. She didn't think she'd have time to line up a final shot before the smaller bugbear showed up and sent her plummeting to the forest floor, so she dismissed the Slinger 300 back into her bag of holding and reached for the vine that she'd originally climbed to get up here.

Unfortunately, before she could even get a solid wrap with one leg on the vine, the zombie bugbear finally arrived at her branch, and she had not yet come up with anything resembling a new strategy.

The branch creaking ominously was her only warning as she hurried to get her legs into position around the vine and started to lower herself. Heading towards the forest floor with the rest of the bugbear zombies was not going to be a healthy decision in her life, but sticking around to get grabbed by a bugbear, or to fall from the full height of her branch, were two certain ways to die. At least lowering at her own speed gave her a *chance* of surviving, even if it was only a small one.

She'd made it substantially less than halfway down the vine when the bugbear pursuing her shifted far enough onto the branch that it split with a crack that sounded like a lightning strike.

Then Lyra experienced that brief moment of weightlessness that always happens just before falling.

"Fuck," she muttered as gravity caught her and pulled.

She really did *not* want to die at the hands of a bunch of undead bugbears at *any* time, but she was particularly angry that she was going to die by zombie bugbear in the middle of *a date*.

When she thought of all the terrible puns her friends would be sure to coin while mourning her, she almost wanted to laugh, but she was far too busy screaming at gravity.

Soon her vision was a blur of limbs, claws, and clubs that swung wildly at her as she clung pointlessly to her vine and fell to her death. She figured it didn't really matter if it was a bugbear or the ground that got her in the end; she'd be dead either way. Though there would be some satisfaction if she managed to take one more bugbear zombie with her at least.

At the last moment, as she fell, she leaned towards one of the shapes that rushed to meet her, hoping it was a zombie that deserved a swift release from its necromantic prison and not the poor cursed chest wrapped in vines. She was certain it wasn't Gwen—she'd have noticed the glowing purple of the ethereal panther—but she couldn't tell what she'd aimed at, or even if she'd hit her mark, before blackness took her.

LYRA BLINKED. THE blackness that had taken her did not appear to be death. Not that she could see much of it from where she was hanging; everything was more of a shapeless golden blur from here, but she could smell it, and… well, she supposed if she'd made it to one of the hells it might smell like molten metal mixed with feces, but… it wasn't a hell she'd ever heard of before. Also, it seemed she was still clinging on to her vine, and she couldn't quite fathom why the vine would have come with her into the afterlife.

"Lyra, is that you?"

Lyra blinked again, and this time she looked down. Just below her was Kiara, standing on a very tiny pile of gold coins, surrounded by a veritable sea of molten metal, with her arms up as if she'd just been casting.

"Kiara?" Lyra asked, still a bit confused about whether or not she was dead. "Where are we?"

"You've already forgotten our picnic?" Kiara asked, with a bemused note to her voice.

"*This* is the cursed chest?"

"I admit, I did some redecorating while you were gone."

"I can see that." It looked like Kiara had been melting as much of the gold in the small pocket dimension as she could and…

"Why does it smell like a cesspit in here?" Lyra asked, wanting to cover her nose but not yet willing to release the vine in her hands.

Kiara's grey skin darkened, and she looked away and coughed.

"I was trying to get the chest to spit me out. I melted as much of the gold as I could first, but when that didn't seem to be working I got a little bit desperate, and I figured if I made it truly awful in here…"

Lyra nodded, understanding and disgust fighting for dominance on her face.

"Right. Ok. That makes… a certain kind of sense, um… want to get out of here?"

Kiara snapped her gaze back to Lyra's and frowned. "How?"

Lyra smiled and gestured to the vine she held. She had no idea how the cursed chest had managed to swallow her without hurting her, or if it had even *meant* to do it—maybe it had just opened its mouth at the opportune moment—but the vine she'd been clinging to even as she fell hadn't dropped her yet, so… "This vine is somehow still attached to a massive branch outside. It's probably on the ground, and likely crawling with zombies, but it's big enough that it should be able to hold us both. Would you like to go first?"

K IARA DID NOT, in fact, want to go first.

She wanted desperately to make sure that Lyra was not going to be trapped down here with Kiara's already-digested dinner and twenty pools of molten gold. Kiara would have been sweating buckets if her greatcoat hadn't been enchanted to regulate her body temperature. Even *with* her greatcoat, her face and hands were slick with sweat. It was bound to be incredibly uncomfortable for Lyra, who had nothing to protect her. But when Kiara had tried to insist Lyra go first, Lyra had reminded her that a battle mage was a much better choice for charging recklessly into however many bugbears were still left up there, and that if Lyra tried to go first, she'd likely die horribly.

"And if I wind up trapped down here, you can come get me out later, after you've finished off the remaining zombies. It's not like I'll die of heat and stench. I won't enjoy it, but it probably won't kill me."

Kiara frowned but had to agree.

"How many of them are left?" she asked.

"I don't really know. There were at least six left when I fell from the tree, but one of them was riding that branch with me and I can't imagine that went particularly well for it."

"So maybe five?"

"Assuming I had the count right to begin with... and depending on how many Gwen might have taken out after I fell... oh, and assuming that they haven't called for reinforcements again."

Kiara sighed.

Right. She was definitely going to be running headfirst into an unknown number of enemies. Oh well. An estimate was better than nothing. And the fact that the only ally she had up there was an ethereal who could heal if she got caught in the crossfire was reassuring.

Kiara's gut turned at the idea of causing Gwen pain, but if it was the difference between letting herself or Lyra die, and it happened because she couldn't see where she was firing in self-defense, well... she still hated it, but at least Gwen would be sure to survive. That was something.

"Ok," she nodded. "Let's do this."

Lyra descended the vine in her usual style, but then seemed reluctant to let it go, even when she reached the floor of the cursed chest. Kiara was torn between moving forward to take the vine and just standing there for a while longer just to fill her eyes with the gorgeous café owner who had come back for her. Maybe Lyra was equally inclined to linger, or maybe she just didn't want to release their only way out of this reeking box, but after a brief hesitation, she handed the vine to Kiara.

Kiara did her best not to get distracted by the swoop in her stomach when her fingers brushed Lyra's as she grabbed the vine in both hands and started to climb.

Or tried to.

How in the hells does Lyra do this?

Kiara had made one large hop up and then pulled herself hand over hand and... she was barely three feet off the floor. She tried to reach higher with one arm, but her muscles were already burning. She tried to hook her leg around the vine, the way she'd seen Lyra do it, and only wound up tangling her foot so much that when she fell down, she landed on her ass with one leg still in the air.

"What the fuck?" she wondered aloud.

Lyra was looking down at her and clearly doing her damnedest not to laugh.

Kiara sighed, still lying on her back on a swath of molten gold that probably would have left her with third-degree burns without the protection of her greatcoat.

She watched Lyra swallow a giggle.

"I forgot that you probably haven't spent much time climbing ropes. Or vines, or fabrics. It's almost all in the legs—I could definitely teach you, and it wouldn't even take that long, but... definitely longer than I want to spend down in this melting cesspit."

Kiara laughed and started to struggle to her feet.

"That's fair. What do you suggest instead?"

Lyra reached out a hand to help Kiara up, then she turned and patted her own back. "Mount up, battle mage."

Kiara considered arguing. After all, Lyra was a good deal shorter than she was, and, despite Kiara's pitiful attempt at climbing a vine just now, she wasn't actually weak. She had a fair bit of muscle on her, not to mention thighs and breasts that weren't nearly as waif-like as her full-elf mother would have preferred. But then Kiara remembered how effortlessly Lyra had been climbing, hanging from, and descending the vines in this cursed forest all night, even though most of the vines had probably been trying to kill her all the while. If the woman thought she could carry Kiara on her back, she was probably right, so Kiara simply nodded her agreement and quietly climbed on.

She was very concerned about where to put her hands.

A part of her wanted to wrap them around the front of Lyra's fabulous chest, but that seemed rather forward, since they hadn't even kissed yet.

On the other hand, she really didn't want to strangle the other woman—or grab her anywhere that would interfere with her climbing.

After several fumbled attempts to hold on, Lyra just grabbed Kiara's arms and situated them across her chest anyway. At least Kiara didn't have to deal with the awkwardness of having placed them there herself.

"Ok," Lyra announced once Kiara was situated, "hang tight, try not to strangle me, and when we get to the top, feel free to throw some fireballs to clear the way. After making it this far, I could really do without getting hit by a bugbear club."

"Ha! Yeah. That would not be my idea of a good time either."

Kiara could barely believe how easy Lyra made it look; climbing that vine with a whole extra person on her back.

It wasn't that the other woman didn't seem strained at all; her forearms were bulging, Kiara could feel the muscles pressed up against her flexing, and Lyra was quickly covered in a solid sheen of sweat. But, Og's Balls, she moved so fluidly, every movement of her arms was smooth and measured. Kiara couldn't tell what Lyra was doing with her legs, exactly, but whatever it was barely jostled her as she clung to the woman's chest.

But as fluidly as Lyra moved, their ascent took longer than Kiara would have expected.

From inside the chest it had only looked like there was about twenty feet of vine dangling into the open space above, but they'd cleared the visible part of the vine after three "climbs"—or whatever Lyra was doing (which, as far as Kiara could tell, was to grab the vine as high as she could reach, hold still while raising her legs up and wrapping them around the vine, then stand up using whatever tenuous hold her feet had and start all over again). Lyra had probably completed four more repetitions of that climb before Kiara could finally see light above them, and it was another four climbs before Kiara was eye-level with that light.

Given how much Lyra was sweating by the time they reached the top, Kiara was very glad they didn't have to go any farther.

Kiara had decided less than halfway up that she would get off of Lyra's back as soon as she could manage it without getting either of them killed. She didn't think that the way her arms and legs were wrapped around Lyra's chest and hips was making it any easier for the café owner to breathe.

So she was ready with a playing card between her fingers the moment that their heads pulled even with the lid of the chest. Kiara released Lyra and clung to the lip of the cursed chest's mouth (or lid, or whatever it was) as she tried to get a look at the fight outside. The opening was only as wide as the vine, about the thickness of Kiara's arm, so she couldn't see all of what was going on out there, but she saw enough.

She flicked her card, fireball side up, and then leapt out after it.

HE RELIEF THAT Lyra felt the moment Kiara launched herself out of the cursed chest and into the battle with the remaining zombified bugbears was short-lived. It was mostly a physical sensation anyway. Her muscles had been burning since about halfway up the damned vine, so as soon as Kiara's weight left her arms she felt light enough to fly.

But there was nowhere to fly to.

Through the small opening of the cursed chest's lid she could see a mass of flaming bugbear, raging panther, and pissed-off battle mage, with little space for a bewildered café owner who moonlighted in a burlesque troupe.

Then she noticed the rapidly increasing heat and stench wafting up from beneath her feet.

Also, there were noises.

They weren't good noises.

The noises emanated from beneath her, or possibly from all around her; she wasn't sure in that moment. It sounded like a very sick cat, or perhaps a raccoon, that had just finished a week-long bender.

They were noises that gave Lyra the distinct impression that she should be elsewhere, quickly.

So she took two more heartbeats to watch the swirl of arms, legs, clubs and claws in front of her, pretending that what she was about to do was just a well-timed aerial move, and not probable suicide by zombie. She pushed the lid open wide enough for her to slide through, then rolled, scrambled, and ran until she was clear of the immediate fight.

It felt like a miracle when she made it to the trees just beyond the tiny clearing where the cursed chest was surrounded by a handful of bugbear zombies.

It even looked like a miracle, Lyra thought, somewhat distractedly, as an intense golden glow rose up through the cursed chest's… mouth? Lid? Opening?

And then, she had just enough time to shout an incoherent warning to Gwen and Kiara, before it looked nothing like a miracle and everything like molten gold and super-heated feces getting sprayed over the entirety of the little clearing.

Chapter Eleven
Exit Strategy

"That. Was. Disgusting," Kiara said, when the chest was finally still. "But I suppose I shouldn't complain."

Kiara looked around her, and was amazed to see that *all* of the remaining bugbears had been coated in enough molten gold and… other… substances to put them down and keep them down.

She barely even saw a twitch from the various bodies that were piled around them.

What was truly amazing, now that Kiara had time to notice, was that neither she nor Gwen had gotten even a drop of the molten metal on them.

She couldn't fathom why, or how, but it seemed like the cursed chest had spared them on purpose.

She wanted to dismiss it as coincidence, but she and Gwen had been in the midst of fighting the bugbears, and it wasn't as though they'd been conveniently placed to one side where the cursed chest might have missed them by chance. No, there were fallen, gold-shrouded zombies on all sides, with two pockets of safety between them. And Lyra… panic seized Kiara for a moment, but then she caught motion in her peripheral vision and saw that Lyra was alive, free, and well enough to be climbing yet another vine.

Kiara let out the breath she'd held without thinking.

"Um… thanks, by the way," she said, turning to the cursed chest.

She wasn't sure if it understood spoken language, but it seemed rude not to say anything.

The chest simply let out a molten burp and flapped its lid closed in what Kiara decided to interpret as a nod.

"See anything good?" Kiara asked in the direction of the canopy, where Lyra had just reached a fairly large tree limb and seemed to be hauling herself up to sit on it.

While Kiara waited for a reply, she looked carefully around her feet and tried to find a safe place to walk. Of course, she didn't have to try too hard because her boots were enchanted enough to protect her from getting burned.

The feces though… well, let's just say she didn't want to test her spellcraft on it.

Gwen, in the nature of large felines everywhere, had simply launched herself from the circle of gold that surrounded her and onto the nearest tree branch overhanging the small clearing, despite that branch being nearly thirty feet up.

"Cats," Kiara muttered, smiling.

"I think I see the trail!" Lyra called.

Kiara's smile faltered.

She desperately wanted to be free of this cursed forest, but she felt a small pang at thinking their date was nearly over. A little voice in her mind suggested that Lyra would probably never want to see her again after this ridiculous experience. She tried to shake the thought away, but it refused to leave.

She cleared her throat and did her best to summon the relief she knew she should have felt.

"Great," she lied. "Let's see if it will actually lead us the hells out of here."

YRA LED GWEN and Kiara through the dark, mist-shrouded forest, dodging wriggling vines, carnivorous plants, and the occasional terrifying insect, towards the small trail that they'd been following what seemed like months ago. Had it really only been a few hours since this date had started?

Of course, Gwen didn't really need leading. She could probably get them out of the cursed forest on her own if Lyra hadn't spotted the trail, but she seemed happy enough plodding along beside them for the moment.

In the companionable silence they shared, with the smell of heated feces and zombie bugbears finally fading into the distance, Lyra almost found the bustling sounds of the cursed forest and the cloying scent of its curse-laden mist comforting.

Wow, Lyra, get it together. This forest is still trying to kill you, and there could be more zombie bugbears at any moment.

To everyone's surprise, the cursed chest was slithering along on its vines behind them too.

Lyra didn't *trust* the creature, precisely. It *had* swallowed her whole—twice—after all. But she was half-convinced it had actually been trying to help both of those times, and besides, what was she going to do, tell it to stay in the cursed forest like some kind of abandoned puppy? That was too cruel to even contemplate.

Kiara must have come to a similar conclusion, and they'd shared a look and both shrugged when it had been clear that the chest meant to follow them.

You like her, don't you? Gwen's voice asked slyly in her head.

Lyra shot a quick glance at Kiara and could tell from the woman's blank expression that Gwen wasn't talking to both of them.

So what if I do? It doesn't matter. Once the adrenaline wears off, she'll remember what a wreck I was inside the cursed chest and she'll never want to see me again. Besides, unless Auryl has a very convincing story to tell me when we get back to the café, I can't, in good conscience, let them operate out of my broom cupboard. Which means no help with rent. Which means I am far *too busy for a girlfriend.*

Gwen said nothing, but, being a cat, she didn't need to. Lyra could feel the disapproval rolling off of her in waves.

I take it you like *her then?* Lyra asked silently.

She doesn't think that ethereal familiars get a very good deal, and that's why she doesn't have one. Besides you and your aunt, she's the only person from this realm I've ever met who feels that way.

Lyra thought about that for a moment. She wasn't certain when Gwen and Kiara would have had the time to discuss the ethical question of familiars, but Lyra had to admit it was very refreshing to meet someone who considered ethereals people, and thought they were being ill-used by magekind.

Well, you're *welcome to date her if you feel that strongly about it.* Lyra worked very hard to keep a straight face while she directed the thought at Gwen.

Gwen swatted lazily at her with a paw that was big enough to cover her entire head, and Lyra just managed to duck while laughing uncontrollably.

"What are you two on about now?" Kiara asked, her eyes sparkling with either curiosity or barely contained mischief.

"Gwen was just explaining to me how it's possible for panthers to fall in love with elves."

The next enormous paw that swatted in her direction made contact, and Lyra tumbled onto the path, still laughing.

Pesky mortal.

"Overgrown house cat!"

Kiara stood between the two of them with her hands on her hips and deadpanned, "If you two don't knock it off, I will turn this cursed chest right back around and abandon you in the cursed forest."

There was one quiet moment during which Gwen and Lyra both stared at her with wide eyes, and then all three of them dissolved into gut-wrenching laughter.

Which lasted until the cursed chest let out a small shriek that had everyone instantly ready to fight.

L YRA FELT HER jaw drop, and could understand why the chest had cried out.

Before them was a stunning scene. A giant sheet of crystalline water turned white with froth cascaded over a cliff that was as tall as some of the trees she'd been climbing all evening. The trail that they were following had swung sharply around a bend, revealing this waterfall and the river that flowed from it, which seemed like it should have been in the midst of a deep canyon and not at all in the middle of a seemingly flat forest.

It didn't make any sense with the lay of the land they'd been following, so Lyra had to assume it was either part of the cursed forest's own magic, or else part of Auryl's spell still at work. She knew that the little dragon's protection was no longer active, but maybe this was part of whatever magic would let them find the portal out of here.

"It's breathtaking," Kiara whispered.

Lyra could only nod in agreement.

Gwen had ignored all of their gasping and exclaiming and simply trotted over to the river's edge in order to have a drink.

Tastes normal enough for all that it looks like an enchantment, she informed them.

"Oh, does... does this trail go where I think it does?" Lyra asked, her voice barely above a whisper. She'd been staring at the waterfall, mesmerized, wishing she could reach out and touch it somehow, even though they were nowhere near enough for that. But now she'd noticed that the trail curved pretty sharply just *before* it reached the cliff face, where it disappeared from view behind a curtain of falling water.

"Dag's tits, I think it does," Kiara replied, her voice almost as awestruck as Lyra's.

Do we trust that the small dragon meant for the date to end on a romantic note, or do we think that there is another group of zombies waiting to kill us behind the falls?

Kiara and Lyra both laughed, and then Lyra realized the panther might not be joking.

"Ever the optimist, Gwen," Lyra said, stepping forward.

She was tempted to grab Kiara's hand as she walked past her, but decided not to push her luck. If the battle mage was preparing to reject her as soon as they got back to Dryvenvale, there was no need to speed things up. "I suppose there's only one way to find out."

So Lyra led them down the trail that followed the gentle curve of a river that should never have been there, then turned sharply to lead them behind a magical waterfall, and, hopefully, back home.

F OR JUST A moment, as the woods before them had gotten noticeably brighter, the air less suffused with mist and the smell of rot, and the whole space had started to feel less… cursed, Lyra had seemed to take a moment to enjoy the view, and Kiara had thought she was going to reach for her hand. Then the moment passed, and Lyra was walking ahead of her.

The entire stretch of trail that led from the cursed forest up to the cliff face with the enormous, magnificent, and hopefully curse-free waterfall clearly didn't belong anywhere near here, and Kiara found it equal parts disturbing and beautiful. But when the final bit of trail turned, gloriously, so that it led between the waterfall and the cliff face, Kiara was so enchanted by the setting that she finally let go of her worries that it was some kind of trap. Mostly.

It wasn't the first time that Kiara had found herself behind a waterfall, but it was probably the first time she'd explored behind one while pining after a woman who was within arm's reach.

Maybe it was just the way that Lyra watched the power of that much water jetting over a cliffside, or maybe it was that the space was dark and close and free of bugbears, or maybe it was just the falls' deafening rush that was somehow soothing… but Kiara found her imagination drawn entirely too quickly to the idea of reaching out to fold Lyra into her arms, and then placing a thousand gentle kisses across her face and neck and… She mentally pinched herself and tried to remember that there was a nine-hundred-pound ethereal panther playing chaperone right now. Not to mention a cursed chest that had eaten them once and… yeah. *Time to calm down, Mefysta.*

There is no need to restrain yourself on my behalf, battle mage. What Lyra does with her love life is her affair. If you ever purposefully harmed her, you might disappear very quickly and quietly with no one on this plane aware of your departure, but barring that, you have nothing to fear from me.

Kiara swallowed, not thrilled with the idea that the enormous panther could go poking around inside her head whenever she wanted to, and also unsure if that last statement had been a threat or not.

Oh, don't look so put off, battle mage. I can't read your thoughts without your permission. And even if I could, that would be unspeakably rude. But your face is as readable as a child's tale, and you smell of wanting besides.

Kiara couldn't help it then; she laughed.

"What?" Lyra asked, her eyes still wide in wonder as she spun in circles, trying to take in every detail of the waterfall and the cave behind it.

"Oh, Gwen is just making fun of me," Kiara said, stepping closer to Lyra and feeling her face splitting into what she was certain was a dopey grin. "And also, you're wonderful."

Lyra's expression shifted from awe to mild surprise. Kiara felt her stomach do a flip.

"Um... would you mind terribly if I kissed you?" Kiara asked, trying not to wince at how damnably formal she sounded. *Yes, very romantic, Ki. Very smooth, very normal, that's definitely how most people talk.*

"I would not," Lyra whispered, stepping a bit closer to Kiara. "Mind, that is. I would not mind."

Kiara was relieved that Lyra seemed to be just as nervous as she was, but before she had more than a second to think about it, she had closed the gap between them and Lyra was right there, and all Kiara had to do was lower her head, and then their lips were touching, and Kiara decided now would be a perfect time for her brain to *shut up.*

L YRA WAS SURE that something terrible must be about to happen, because this was obviously too good to be true.

Maybe Kiara was just kissing her for fun because they were standing under a waterfall and it was unbelievably romantic, and my gods, how could you NOT? Or else there were more zombies lurking around the next bend who were about to kill them before they'd even finished their kiss.

Which would be criminal, if you asked Lyra, because this kiss was warming her all the way to the tips of her toes, and she was already having some delightful ideas about other areas of Kiara's anatomy that she'd like to kiss and... oh dear. She really hoped Kiara wasn't doing this as some strange prelude to them never seeing each other again, because she very much wanted to discover what else this woman's tongue could do. Wow.

After much longer than Lyra had expected, but quite a bit less time than she *wanted*, Kiara stepped back from the kiss.

"I'm sorry, I um... got a bit carried away there. But I'd really like to do that again sometime, if you umm... would like?"

Lyra found herself laughing at how polite the battle mage's words were.

"I would *very* much like to do that again," Lyra admitted. "In fact, I'm rather upset that we've stopped."

Lyra wasn't sure, because Kiara's grey skin didn't flush in the same shades as her own purple tones did, but she was fairly certain the battle mage was blushing.

"I'm sorry about stopping, I just... I got worried that the bugbears might show up, or the portal could close or... well, it just seems safer if we get out of here sooner than later."

Lyra felt her own cheeks flushing then. Gods, she'd been the one thinking about how awful it would be if there were bugbears waiting around the next bend to kill them all not a minute ago. Of course they should be going. Especially since she knew that the original protection spell that was meant to be keeping them safe for the duration of their "date" was no longer effective. Gods, she should have been rushing them out of here the moment they found the trail, not fantasizing about taking Kiara up against the cliff side like some kind of reckless school girl.

"Right," Lyra said, swallowing her own longing. "Let's get out of here and then try that again, shall we?"

If you're both done with your strange two-legged mating rituals, I believe I've found the portal that leads back to Lyra's café.

Lyra and Kiara shared a brief embarrassed smile, but Lyra was still enjoying the heat of their kiss and she didn't even mind Gwen's teasing. She just gestured towards the back of the cave and followed after Kiara.

Sure enough, tucked behind a boulder that was almost as large as Gwen herself, they found a blue swirling portal that matched the one they'd passed through to get here.

"So... who wants to go first?" Kiara asked.

She, Lyra, and Gwen were all still staring at each other when the cursed chest pushed its uncountable vine limbs between them and shoved its way into the portal.

"Um…" said Kiara.

"Oh dear…" agreed Lyra.

Well, fuck, said Gwen. *I suppose we'd better go after it.*

And with that, all three of them piled into the portal as quickly as they could.

Chapter Twelve
Party Debrief

Lyra wasn't sure what she'd expected upon their triumphant return, but all three of them being crammed into the dark broom cupboard, getting slapped by dozens of writhing vines and an enormous purple panther tail, was not it.

"Why are we all still in the cupboard?" she asked, as soon as she stepped out of the portal and walked directly into Kiara's greatcoat-covered back.

She wasn't entirely sure if she'd actually bounced off of Kiara's back or if the greatcoat itself had repelled her. The thing was clearly spelled seven ways to Solday, and she wasn't convinced it would allow her to do anything as uncouth as bounce off its owner.

She'd been half certain while she and Kiara had been kissing that the coat had been gently pushing her back, as though she were an errant fireball (not one big enough to be a real threat). Well, she could hardly blame the coat for the mistake; she *had* felt a bit like a fireball during that kiss.

Down, Lyra, you're still in the broom cupboard.

A tiny voice cleared its throat behind her.

"Glad to see you, yes!" chirped Auryl from the shelf behind Lyra's shoulder.

She turned around to see the tiny dragon standing on two legs, looking up at them eagerly. She thought the concern in their voice was genuine but….

"*You,*" growled Kiara, whipping around fast as a snake. "You could have killed us!"

Luckily, Lyra was already between the dragon and the battle mage, because the look on Kiara's face was not one that promised good judgment.

Auryl glanced at Lyra, looking surprisingly nervous, and she wondered if the tiny dragon actually expected her to protect them.

"Well," Auryl explained when Lyra didn't interject, "for most of it, there was really no danger. It was only after the protection spell broke when Lyra was ejected from the portal that put you in peril—but Lyra was very brave!"

"She—wait, what?" Kiara looked between Auryl and Lyra, and Lyra felt the urge to cover her face.

"Um... there wasn't really time for me to fill everyone in on that part, Auryl, what with… one thing and another."

Of course there *had* been time after they'd finally fought their way free of the zombies, but by that point Lyra had been too busy thinking about kissing Kiara to remember the whole mortal peril thing and Auryl's spell and... well, everything.

Honestly, the whole part where she had been sent back to the café seemed like the least real portion of the whole date.

"Well, the important thing is—" but the tiny dragon was interrupted by a small, though still earsplitting, shriek, before they could elucidate anyone on the important thing.

Everyone turned towards the door to the broom closet, where a few flailing vines were all that Lyra could see of the cursed chest given that there were nine hundred pounds of panther and a battle mage between them.

"Chester?" chirped the tiny dragon. "Chester, what in all the realms are *you* doing here?"

The cursed chest, who was apparently named Chester, flailed its vines and shrieked rather plaintively. Auryl sighed. They waved a small taloned finger in the air, and the door to the broom cupboard popped open. Without any hesitation at all, the cursed chest surged through the doorway and out into the café.

"What in the nine hells is THAT!?" cried a voice that Lyra recognized.

Gwen, ever dignified, was not to be rushed, but even moving at her most dignified pace, it didn't take her long to get out of the broom cupboard, and suddenly there was quite a bit more space for everyone else.

Not that Lyra had time to enjoy the newfound room to breathe; she needed to go make sure that Chester didn't hurt her friends, or that her friends didn't hurt Chester. And she was 99% certain that the voice that had cried out a second ago wasn't Sylvan's.

K IARA WAS ALREADY moving before anyone outside the broom cupboard had time to scream, but she didn't let that squeal slow her down. The voice had been raised several octaves higher than she was used to hearing it, but she could have sworn that it was a voice she recognized…

Sure enough, when she stepped into the calming amber light of the café, she saw a familiar face standing on a small table, looking like a very startled statue of an elven god.

"Kyle?"

The statue turned to her.

"Ki?"

Lyra pushed past her and ran farther into the room, looking between Chester, who was flailing rather desperately at the door to the street, and Kyle, who was still standing on the table as if it were his plinth.

"Kyle? What are you doing here?" Lyra asked.

Kyle, who somehow managed to look beautiful even while cowering on a café table, frowned.

"You didn't come home. I was worried. And when I decided to come check on you, Sylvan was still here and told me I could join her while we waited for you."

Lyra sighed. Kiara frowned.

"Come home?" Kiara repeated, her mind whirling through the various possible puzzle pieces that would fit this particular gap.

Lyra smiled and walked over to offer Kyle her hand so that he could descend from the café table without toppling it.

"Oh, sorry," she said, turning to look over her shoulder at Kiara even while she still held Kyle's hand. "Introductions! Right. Kyle, this is Kiara, my date. Kiara, this is Kyle, my roommate."

Kiara would have laughed, but she was busy piecing together a few more details.

"We've met," said Kyle, in a monotone that gave nothing away, and now Kiara *did* laugh.

"Met? Kyle, that's a bit of an understatement. We grew up together!"

Apparently, it was Lyra's turn to look shocked. But Kiara couldn't let go of one last detail.

"Kyle, you said your roommate was a fellow dancer?"

Kyle nodded, face still inscrutable.

"From your burlesque troupe?" Kiara continued, unable to stop herself.

Lyra turned and her eyes met Kiara's, her expression wary, as if she was expecting to be hurt at any moment.

"I hadn't gotten around to mentioning that part yet, but I did tell you I was a dancer."

Oh, Kiara could tell that Lyra must have shared some of Kyle's hurt, either because Kyle had shared his own family torment with her, or because she had cretins of her own to deal with, but Kiara knew she wasn't going to let that hurt look linger if she could help it.

"To be very clear," she said, before anyone could get, or keep, the wrong idea. "Unlike ninety percent of my ridiculous family, I have nothing against Kyle's chosen profession or anyone else who works in the industry. I'm just surprised because I'd always thought Kyle's roommate was a man. Not that he'd ever said that, but I don't know… I just sort of assumed…" she trailed off, not sure what else to say. She didn't even know *why* she'd made that assumption, she just always had. Maybe because Kyle had told her so many stories of how uncomfortable most women made him feel?

"So, you're not opposed to dating someone who regularly flashes her breasts at a paying audience?" Lyra asked, clearly wanting to get to the heart of the matter.

Kiara answered without hesitation. "I have no right to dictate what anyone flashes at anyone else, as long as everyone consents. And I would be honored to date *you* no matter who you flash your breasts at." Then she turned on Kyle. "I really wish that I'd ignored Aunt Demalca's embargo on seeing your shows ages ago, Kyle. If I'd known your troupe-mates were gorgeous women who drop sewing machines on zombies without batting an eye, I would have specifically rescheduled some of my missions for that express purpose."

Finally, Kyle smiled.

"So you *do* recognize how spectacular she is."

Kiara smiled back.

"Of course."

"And you've decided you're not above romantic entanglements after all?" he asked.

Kiara frowned. She and Kyle had bonded the past few times they'd been thrown together at family affairs, as the only remaining unattached members of their generation. All of their siblings and cousins had spouses or long-term partners, and while Kyle had never been interested in romance *at all*, Kiara had simply sworn it off after her last disastrous relationship.

"I wish I were more like you in that regard, Coz, but I'm afraid Est was right all along. I've been missing the romance, despite what I've been telling myself for the past five years."

To Kiara's surprise and relief, Kyle smiled even brighter at that.

"Ha! She owes me thirty gold pieces!"

"What? Why?"

"Because you admitted you missed romance before anyone had to hit you over the head with a brick!"

And Kiara couldn't help herself: at that, she cackled.

L YRA SIDLED QUIETLY across the hardwood floor and woven carpets that covered the space between the broom cupboard and the door to the street, and tried her best *not* to look like she was paying close attention to the conversation between Kyle and Kiara.

But come on.

Kyle was Kiara's *cousin?*

And they were talking about Kiara's ex?

It would take a stronger will than Lyra's to ignore *that* conversation.

"I was afraid Evain had ruined you," Kyle was saying now.

Lyra reached the door to her shop and managed to dodge through the flailing vines of the cursed chest to reach the lock above the door. After using her key to release the latch, she pulled the door handle and allowed Chester to wiggle and slide its way out the door and into the street.

She had to hope that Chester wasn't going to wander around eating people wherever it went. She liked to believe that it wouldn't, but she also just didn't want the poor creature breaking down her door in its attempts to get out, and no one else seemed to be paying the poor thing any attention.

She watched as the cursed chest made its way down the darkened sidewalk in front of her shop and turned the corner at the end of her block. She thought that maybe one of the tentacle vines had waved at her as the creature slipped into the darkness, but it could have been her imagination.

"Est was certain she had, but I don't think that's fair to Evain. For all her problems, she never forced me to shove my head so far up my ass that I saw my own spine. I did that all on my own."

Lyra turned around to find Kyle blinking at his cousin.

She also finally took a good look at Sylvan, who stood behind the counter, where she'd been casually wiping mugs ever since they'd first burst out of the broom cupboard, as though the tauryn saw enormous cursed chests wrapped in so many vines you couldn't even tell they were chest-shaped wandering through the café every morning—unlike Kyle, who had used all his elven grace and hard-won strength to launch himself on top of the nearest table the moment the strange creature had passed through the door.

Kyle was now the picture of careless contemplation as he leaned against that same table and stared at his cousin.

"That's quite a bit more clarity than I expected you to have on the matter," Kyle admitted, as Lyra made her way back to the conversation, or at least to the place where the conversation was happening.

"Well, I was wrong about it for a very long time. It seems like a waste to keep going now."

"But how did you even..." Kyle trailed off, clearly uncomfortable with finishing the sentence.

"Pull my own head OUT of my ass?" Kiara offered, and Lyra couldn't help but chuckle; Kiara's voice was so matter-of-fact she might as well have been ordering coffee. "One heart-to-heart with Lyra, and too much time trapped in a cursed chest by myself, finally did the trick."

Lyra, no longer able to handle the feeling that she was missing something, raised her hand.

Kyle played along and pointed to her, saying in his most bored academic voice, "Yes, Lyra. Question?"

"What in the hells are you two talking about?"

Kiara sighed and rubbed her forehead. "My ex," she muttered.

"And your own stupidity. Don't forget that part."

"Yes. Thank you, Kyle."

"Always happy to help, Coz."

"Not sure I like your definition of *help*, Coz."

Lyra cleared her throat and enjoyed the unsettling experience of having both Kiara and Kyle give her their full attention at the same time.

"Wow, ok. Now see, when you do *that*, I wonder how I never guessed you were Kyle's cousin."

Lyra had to fight back a laugh when Kiara and Kyle gave her matching blinks of confusion.

"Never mind. Look. My real question is, while I understand that there's an ex involved, you both seem to be talking about some weird hurdle that Kiara has overcome. But I can't for the life of me figure out what that hurdle is."

Kiara's grey skin darkened slightly at her neck and the tips of her long pointed ears, and Lyra decided that was *definitely* a blush.

"Care to fill me in?" she asked.

"I umm… I don't date," Kiara muttered.

Lyra tilted her head to one side.

"All evidence to the contrary," Lyra said, wondering if she'd somehow just hallucinated the past few hours of her life, or if this was just the preamble to Kiara walking away from her now that they were no longer fighting for their lives at every turn.

"No. I mean, it's… I made an exception for tonight because… well, it's a long story, but… generally speaking, I don't date."

"Then what is the ex you were talking about?" Lyra could feel her own cheeks warming as she realized that all of her worst fears were coming true in front of her. *This is it, this is the part where she tells me I'm too broken and walks away. Damn it all, why did that kiss have to be so good? I wasn't expecting this test run of Auryl's matchmaking service to lead to anything, but I let that damned kiss get my head all fuzzy.*

"She's *why* I don't date."

"Ha! See. I told you—" Kyle began to interrupt but Kiara cut him off.

"No. I mean, she's the one who made it perfectly clear that it was wrong for someone in my line of work to expect anyone to put up with the risks of being with me."

Kyle snorted derisively from beside Lyra, and she tried to take comfort in the fact that Kyle also seemed to think this was horseshit.

"I thought we already established that you were more likely to get killed walking to the Guild hall than fighting monsters?" Lyra didn't know why she was even arguing at this point. She should have just been letting Kiara walk on her merry way, but the idea was just so *stupid.*

Kiara took a deep breath and then put on a very weak smile. "You're right, and honestly, I should have known that five years ago, when Evain told me that she couldn't be expected to wait around for someone like me to find a real job that wouldn't risk me dying and leaving a family behind. But, I guess… everything she said was all stuff I'd thought of myself and… well, I think it was easier to believe that my job was a legitimate problem than to admit to myself that I'd spent years of my life with someone who didn't actually love me."

"I'm sure your family harping on and on about how 'if you were a real mage you'd be doing research in Terithlan' didn't help," Kyle supplied helpfully.

Kiara laughed and rolled her eyes.

"Gods, don't remind me. Yes, that too."

Lyra would have been shocked to hear that Kiara's family didn't think working for the Adventurer's Guild as a battle mage was a lofty enough profession, except that she had known Kyle for years now and she was well aware of how backwards some of *his* family's views were. Apparently, he and Kiara shared that wonderful bit of inheritance.

"So, Kyle's family disowned him for becoming an exotic dancer, and yours disowned you for using your magic to fight monsters and save lives?"

"That about sums it up, yes. Only it's basically all the same family, so it should really come as no surprise to anyone."

Lyra pulled out a chair from one of her small tables and turned towards the counter where Sylvan was *still* standing, drying more mugs, even though Lyra was fairly certain that all the mugs had already been clean *before* she had left on her date.

"Syl, my dear friend, we are going to need an entire round of cappuccinos. Would you be so very kind as to get the machine running?"

"Yes, boss."

"Do NOT call me that."

"Ok, boss."

"Syl!"

"I'm just teasing, but you're paying me overtime for this."

"Of course I am. And as soon as the machine is on, I'll make the cappuccinos while you keep these two on topic." Then she turned to Kiara and Kyle, who were both pulling out chairs to join her at the table. "Now, then," she said, looking from one to the other of them. "Who the fuck is this Evain, and why didn't you let Kyle slap some sense into her?" Lyra asked with a grin.

KIARA LET THE sounds of three enthusiastic friends arguing wash over her as she allowed her eyes to wander over the interior of Lyra's cozy little café. She was finally feeling the exhaustion of the past few hours now that her mind had finally accepted that they were safe, and it was making her a bit drowsy. Or maybe that was just because this place smelled of Lyra: coffee beans, pastries, and the lemon water they obviously used to clean things.

Kiara couldn't help but smile, thinking that most people would probably consider it the opposite, believing that Lyra smelled like the café, but Kiara knew that after the dozens of times she'd had her face pressed into the woman's hair, or her shoulder, or her lips, over the past few hours she would always think of that combination of scents as Lyra's and not the café's.

This rather ridiculous line of thought was abruptly interrupted as Kiara caught the sight of something small, green, and purple slip past her peripheral vision.

She made a point of getting up slowly so as not to interrupt the flow of conversation. They had all been getting up to refill their coffees as the initially awkward conversation about Kiara's past relationships had drifted on to other topics, including the fascinating tale of why Sylvan, Lyra's best friend and employee, had vowed to mule-kick both of Lyra's exes should they ever make the unfortunate choice to show their faces where Sylvan could see them—a plan that Gwen, curled up beside Lyra's chair and taking up just as much space as the other four together, fully, and vocally, approved of.

Between all the coffee refills and bathroom breaks, no one reacted when Kiara rose from her seat, and she made it as far as the hearth in the widest part of the café before the tiny dragon seemed to realize they were being followed.

"You need something, Mage Mefysta?" Auryl squeaked.

"Lyra and the others might have forgotten you in all the chaos of making it out of that debacle alive, but this isn't my first time escaping a dungeon I didn't expect to walk into," Kiara said, trying to keep the edge of anger out of her voice. It wasn't like threatening the dragon would do any good, and what she really wanted was answers.

"Lyra can explain what happened, but you were never meant to be in any danger," Auryl chirped from the floor. "Chester should *not* have been there, but even still, it never would have resulted in my protection spell being broken if Lyra had not touched the ethereal pendant while still inside of Chester."

Kiara stared at the tiny dragon for much longer than was socially acceptable before saying, "So, that's it? You didn't mean to put us in danger, so we have nothing to be upset about? Your intentions trump reality? That's not a very draconic set of ethics, as far as I understand them."

Now the little dragon fluttered up to the top of the nearest leather couch and blinked at Kiara before answering, "It is you two-leggers who are always making allowances for intention, Fire Mage. You know enough of dragon ethics to know we care nothing for intentions and everything for results, yet you think I have something to be sorry for? Let me ask you this, Mage Mefysta, did you die?"

Kiara rolled her eyes and opened her mouth to answer, but the dragon cut her off.

"Were you harmed? Do you have a single cut or injury on your person aside from the type of bruise or scrape you might get in a training session at your Guild?"

When Kiara started to splutter about how that wasn't the point and how wounds didn't have to be physical to be valid, Auryl cut her off again.

"Did you not find an acceptable mate who also finds you to be an acceptable mate, and who, with luck, will make you happy for very many years to come?"

At that, Kiara's mouth snapped shut.

With a satisfied nod, the little dragon jumped off the couch and fluttered to the floor, where it shuffled quietly to the door, which opened with a tiny flick from the dragon's tail.

"Ugh… I hate that they're right," came a voice from behind her.

Kiara nearly jumped out of her skin, but when she turned and found it was just Lyra behind her, with Kyle and Sylvan still chatting animatedly at the table behind them, she couldn't help but smile.

"Which part were they right about?" she asked, wondering how much of that exchange Lyra had heard.

"Well, all of it, but especially that last part," Lyra said, smiling. Then she frowned and her cheeks flushed. "I mean… not that I can promise I'll make you happy for many years to come or anything… that would be weirdly presumptuous, I think, after just one date, but… what I mean is…"

Lyra swallowed and Kiara watched the way her throat moved with more than a little interest.

"What I mean is, by dragon standards, they haven't done anything wrong. It all worked out ok in the end, and we're both better off than we were before we entered their spell bargain, and they know it."

Kiara knew it was important, but she didn't really want to talk about the dragon anymore.

"Hey," she said instead, trying to keep her voice casual. "Remember when we were under that waterfall and we had to stop kissing because we thought zombies might show up to kill us at any moment?"

Lyra's eyes widened slightly, and she took a step closer to Kiara.

Kiara took another step closer to Lyra in turn, and suddenly their bodies were a hair's breadth away from touching.

"Remember how we said we'd do that again as soon as we were somewhere with fewer zombies?"

"Yeah?" Lyra breathed.

Kiara braced herself, but this time she remembered the name of the café *before* she made the cheesiest joke she could think of, "Well, I hate to say it, but… I think we're in the Right Place."

Lyra snorted, then let out a full-throated laugh that made Kiara's stomach drop in the most delightful way. And then they were suddenly together, their lips warm and soft against each other, as they let the rest of the world slip away.

Chapter Thirteen
A Balanced Party

KIARA HAD NEVER been so delighted to be in a crowd of people. The dark theater, filled occasionally with brilliant flashes of light from the stage, the scent of too many people seated far too close, and the sounds of hushed anticipation as the audience awaited the next marvel were not normally things that Kiara enjoyed. But she'd never enjoyed a performance more, and she'd never been so turned on and proud at the same time. It was an odd combination of emotions.

Finally seeing Kyle perform the absolutely bonkers feats of athleticism and grace that he had been training and performing for the past two decades was a special thrill of its own. Not being interested in the male physique in general, and especially not her cousin's, it was easy to ignore the sensuality of his performance and simply be blown away by the sheer physicality of it. He was incredibly flexible, incredibly strong, and he had an excellent sense of rhythm that Kiara had never known about—unsurprising, given how the man refused to dance at every public function he'd ever been invited to. But seeing him now, the way he moved gracefully across the stage with every twitch of his muscles coordinated with the music the pit band was playing below, she couldn't imagine how there was ever a time he wasn't dancing.

But witnessing the talents that had gotten Kyle ostracized from their quirky family was only half the reason that Kiara was here, glued to her seat and waiting between every set with bated breath. She was delighted to rebel against her aunt and uncle's embargo on supporting Kyle's "uncouth professional choices" and would have done so long ago if she hadn't seemed to be on Guild assignments every time he had a performance (honestly, it had gotten to be a running joke that Kyle's parents must somehow be scheduling Guild assignments), but she was even more delighted to support Lyra's first Night Guild show in months. Thanks to Auryl continuing to rent her broom cupboard for their matchmaking service, the café owner could finally afford to hire more employees, and thus take more time for rehearsals and training.

After a few lengthy chats with the tiny dragon, Lyra had decided their services were actually safe for public consumption and that she wouldn't be betraying her customers by letting the little dragon hang their shingle in her establishment. Kiara'd had her own talks with Auryl—finding a horde of zombies in a cursed forest was a Guild-reportable event, whether it happened on a date or in the middle of another assignment, and the Guild chair had requested Kiara lead the follow-up interviews—which was part of why she'd had to leave on assignment so soon after their first date, and also why she'd be leaving again tomorrow on a new assignment, but she was doing her best not to think about that part.

The important bit was that *now*, only three weeks later, Lyra was performing with the Night Guild again, a feat that Kiara had been given to understand was worthy of praise all on its own. Kiara hadn't realized that the Night Guild was the top burlesque troupe in all of Dryvenvale, possibly in all of Tyrlan, until she'd casually mentioned this performance to one of her Guild crew and gotten an earful about how lucky she was to have even gotten tickets.

As Kiara watched the Night Guild troupe go about their business, each member of the troupe either performing solo or in small groups, every act combining a series of aerial acrobatics with sultry music and sometimes even with sensuous vocals, she was so damned impressed with *everyone* that she was having a hard time not clapping or cheering the moment the curtains opened. And she found it a complete and utter struggle not to shout, "That's my date!" every time Lyra appeared on stage for her routines.

The performances were all undeniably sexy, and Kiara appreciated every single woman that made an appearance on stage, whether she wound up baring her breasts or not—Kiara had been delighted to learn that doing so was not obligatory, but rather the choice of each performer, and she was equally delighted with either choice—but Kiara was unsurprised to find that Lyra was by far the most captivating of them all.

And she couldn't help but think that when Lyra descended from a green set of aerial silks in the final act of the show, her body wrapped in a costume made of vines that framed every part of her anatomy in the most alluring way possible, that it was a nod to their first date and a personal note to Kiara.

Of course, it was also the sexiest thing Kiara had ever seen in her life.

She thought she might have applauded louder than anyone else in the entire audience when it was time for the standing ovation at the end. She *might* have been the first person to stand, but she couldn't be sure.

She *was* sure that she was one of the first people to exit the theater and stand in line at the backstage door where the bouncers—a good-sized troll who she thought she recognized from work, and a dwarf with a hammer on her back that was bigger than Lyra—were already waiting to keep back the hordes.

Kiara didn't even mind the crowd piling up behind her as she waited. She had been gone for most of the three weeks since she'd last seen Lyra, and this was the first time they would get to spend together since her assignment.

"Mage Mefysta?" asked the troll, who seemed to have finally recognized her.

"Hey, Flannery," she replied, trying to wipe the goofy smile off her face and failing.

"Are you workin' security for one of the dancers?" Flannery asked.

"Ah… no. Not officially."

"Oh. I didn't take you to be an autograph chaser. No offense," Flannery added belatedly.

Kiara wasn't entirely sure what an autograph chaser was, though she supposed the name was rather descriptive.

"I'm not here for autographs, if that's what you mean," she finally said.

"Well, the dancers don't offer any other servi—"

The troll was cut off by the roar of noise from the crowd behind Kiara as the doors to the backstage opened and a half a dozen performers poured out. Kiara barely even saw the first five of them, because her eyes were drawn and trapped by the purple-skinned, green-haired goddess at the back.

The other dancers all made their way to the crowd, with only occasional interference from the bouncers, signing bits of paper, clothing, and even skin, presented by the adoring crowd.

Lyra, however, walked straight up to Kiara and stood before her.

"Hey," she said, with a shy smile.

"That," Kiara said, her own smile taking over her face, "was the most brilliant performance I have ever seen. Also, the sexiest. But mostly, brilliant. I knew you were good at climbing cursed vines, but you are truly exceptional at moving with those silks! How can you bear to walk on the ground?"

Kiara abruptly shut her mouth because she realized she was babbling, but luckily Lyra took that opportunity to step forward and give her a kiss on the cheek.

"You're adorable, and I'm very happy to see you. Are you ready for our second date?"

Kiara nodded happily.

"Date?" shouted Flannery from a few feet away.

Kiara turned a sheepish grin towards the troll and shrugged.

"Is that a problem, Flannery?" she asked, unsure how else to respond, but relieved to see that the troll was grinning from ear to ear.

"Nah, mate. Not at all. You just won me fifty gold pieces, that's all."

YRA WAS SLIGHTLY baffled by just how many people had apparently placed bets on whether or not Kiara would ever date again, but she decided now was not the time to worry about it. After all, she had been looking forward to this date, hopefully with 100% fewer bugbear zombies, for weeks now. It had been disappointing when she'd learned that Kiara was headed out on a new assignment only a few days after their first date, before they'd even had a chance to see each other again, but Lyra had quickly used the opportunity to dive into training with Night Guild again, now that she could afford to, and the time had passed so quickly she'd hardly felt ready for tonight's performance, let alone seeing Kiara in person once more.

But as she stood in the slightly damp alley, which thankfully smelled of an afternoon rain shower rather than any of the less appealing reasons an alley might be damp, she couldn't help but think that the three weeks apart had only made Kiara seem even more appealing.

She was standing by the theater door chatting amiably with Flannery while they waited, and the light from the lamp above the stage doors lit her white hair in a golden glow that reflected prettily in her purple eyes. But Lyra's favorite part of the whole scene was that Kiara was wearing her leather greatcoat, as always, and the same thigh-high leather boots with stiletto heels that she had worn on their first date.

Would Lyra ever get used to dating a woman that gorgeous, who could also fight off half a dozen bugbears at once?

The backstage door opened and Kyle walked out, along with a few other stragglers that Lyra said goodnight to as she stepped up and linked her arm through Kyle's elbow.

"We're ready," Lyra said to Kiara as they walked up to where she still stood chatting with Flannery.

"Oh right! Game night means we're walking to your place, so I guess it only makes sense to walk with Kyle, too."

Lyra thought that Kiara might be thinking out loud to cover her surprise at seeing Lyra arm in arm with Kyle, but she just chuckled and said, "Please be so kind as to take Kyle's other arm, my dear Fire Mage?"

Kiara looked puzzled, but didn't hesitate to loop her arm through Kyle's other elbow.

Flannery waved them off, and then they wove their way through the last stragglers from the crowd.

As they went, Lyra took on her usual role, doing all she could to keep up a stream of chatter that Kyle laughed at loudly and often, while also touching Kyle more than was strictly necessary and leaning on him periodically. Lyra hoped that Kiara would join in too, as this always worked better with two.

It took Kiara a minute or two to catch on, but after they walked past the third cluster of fans who turned away looking disappointed while Kyle reacted as if he'd never found anyone more entrancing than Lyra and her awkward jokes, Kiara joined the act, fawning over Kyle and casually running her free hand over his shoulder.

When they were seven blocks away from the theater, Kyle finally dropped both their arms and put up the hood of his cloak. "Thank you both. Kindly do not touch me again for another month, at least."

Lyra shifted over so that she was now in the middle and took both their elbows, which Kyle allowed, because they both knew that they couldn't drop the farce entirely until they got home.

"Sorry about that," she muttered to Kiara. "Kyle has more than one stalker, and making it look like he has at *least* two girlfriends is the only safe way to get him away from the theater after a performance."

Kiara winced. "That's awful, Kyle. I'm so sorry. You'd think telling them you're not interested would be more than enough."

Kyle merely shrugged from somewhere in the depths of his very large hood. "Thankfully, I have enough close friends who don't find me the least bit attractive, and whose touch I can tolerate for brief periods of time, to confuse all of the men and women who think I can't possibly be sincere in my rejection if I'm not already romantically entwined with someone else."

Lyra watched a look of horror cross Kiara's face and decided to change the subject.

"So, what are we playing tonight?" she asked.

Kiara smiled, but shrugged, "I have no idea what the options are, so don't ask me."

Kyle nearly cackled with glee as they turned down the final street before their apartment.

"Oooh, Kiara, prepare for me to take vengeance for all those times you forced me to play Word Tiles when we were children!"

Kiara only laughed. "You definitely are owed some sort of recompense for how utterly I destroyed you in those games."

Lyra laughed and let the easy banter between her date and one of her dearest friends wash over her as they walked towards her home.

"You are *both* going to get absolutely demolished by Syl and her partners, so I don't know why you're even plotting against each other; if anything, you should band together in self-defense."

But before the other two could respond they'd reached their building and were piling through the door of Lyra and Kyle's apartment to the warm smell of fresh-baked cookies—most likely courtesy of Syl's partner Enid, the sound of dice rolling against a wooden table, and the gentle teasing of her closest friends welcoming her date into her home.

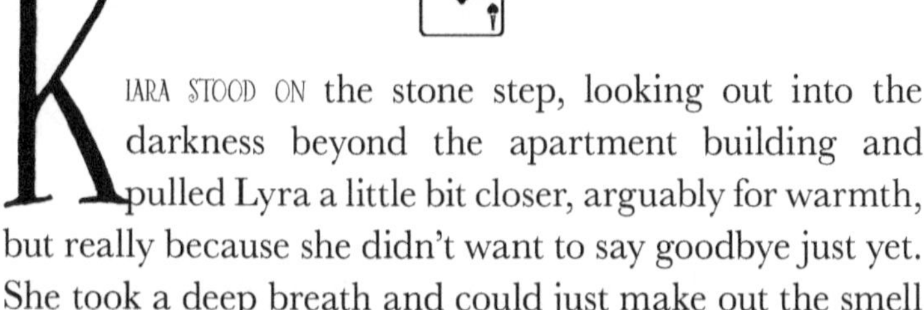

KIARA STOOD ON the stone step, looking out into the darkness beyond the apartment building and pulled Lyra a little bit closer, arguably for warmth, but really because she didn't want to say goodbye just yet. She took a deep breath and could just make out the smell of coffee and pastries over the pervasive smell of wet cobblestones that the recent rains had coated the city in.

When Lyra tilted her head back to look into Kiara's eyes, Kiara couldn't resist leaning down to steal another kiss, and Lyra responded with enthusiasm.

"Your friends are really lovely," Kiara said, when they finally broke apart.

Lyra smiled, and Kiara melted a tiny bit more.

If she didn't want to spend all night on this step—and while part of her very much wanted that as long as Lyra was in her arms the whole time, the rest of her insisted she might die horribly the next day if she didn't get enough sleep—she would need to leave soon, so she made herself say what she'd been thinking all evening.

"I can totally see why Mage Stanglevine felt like... like it would be alright whenever she left you."

Kiara hesitated, not sure that had come out right, but Lyra was only smiling at her with a curious tilt to her lips, so Kiara pressed on.

"I mean, I think you're amazing, and I'm sure you'd be fine no matter who else you had in your life. But... but those friends you've got up there..." Kiara gestured with her chin at the apartment above them, where they'd left Kyle, Syl, and three of Syl's partners debating whether or not there could ever be an ethical form of necromancy. "Those friends are as strong as any adventuring crew. You could take those people into a dungeon with you and know they would have your back, no matter what."

Now Lyra's smile was so big it took up most of her face, and then she was leaning in for another kiss, so Kiara felt obliged to meet her halfway.

"You're right," Lyra said, when they broke apart again. "I do have really good people in my life. And I think Aunt Vi would be delighted that I've recently collected one more."

Kiara's whole chest warmed with that thought.

"I wish I didn't have to go on this next assignment right away," she whispered, her forehead pressed against Lyra's.

Kiara hated this part. The part where she was expected to pretend that she didn't enjoy her work. Or that it wasn't as important as the person she was leaving. This was the part where Evain had always turned sullen and resentful; at first it had just been a teasing pout about how much she would miss Kiara, but eventually it had just been open resentment of Kiara's work. She tried to push those memories away because Lyra was *not* Evain, but she braced herself for it anyway. She couldn't help it.

Lyra only smiled and kissed her cheek, pushing her gently away.

"You'll be back soon," she said, with a delightfully mischievous glint in her eyes.

"Yes, I will."

"And we'll have a third date," Lyra continued, stepping even farther back.

"That would be lovely."

"So, you'd better get going," Lyra insisted, stepping back to the door that led into her building.

Kiara tried not to let her heart plummet at the sight of Lyra stepping away from her, even though she'd just been dreading Lyra trying to keep her here. *Gods, what's wrong with you, Kiara? Make up your mind.*

"So that you can hurry up and get back here!" Lyra finished, jumping from the doorway to plant one more quick kiss on Kiara's lips before turning and running, giggling like a child, all the way back inside her building and slamming the door.

Kiara, suddenly delighted with everything and stumbling in the kind of happy haze reserved for holiday revelers and new lovers, walked back to her room at the Guild hall, only mildly concerned that she might already be falling in love with a woman on only their second date.

Epilogue

AURYL PERCHED ON their favorite shelf in the broom cupboard, basking in the blue-green glow of the portal mirror and letting the flow of their swiftly growing hoard surge through them as yet another happy pair of two-leggers found love in one of Auryl's dungeons. Of course, dungeon was a loose term, as Auryl had explained to the fire mage after the cursed forest debacle. For the purposes of Auryl's magic, it was any place that they confined with their protection spell to have only one entrance and one exit, so long as that place was sufficiently populated with monsters, traps, and other dangers.

It had been a little over one month since Auryl had established their new location here in Dryvenvale, and with at least one couple finding love each day, sometimes with as many as three couples on the busy days, things were going exactly to plan.

Well, things were going exactly to plan as long as they didn't count the minor blip of Lyra and Kiara briefly facing *actual* mortal peril on that test run right at the beginning. But why should they count that? It had all ended well enough, and Chester's presence hadn't wound up being significant in the long run.

A high-pitched buzzing distracted Auryl from their musings, and they turned towards the door to the broom cupboard, already annoyed with whoever wanted their attention. But they opened the door with a flick of their magic anyway.

"Who is being needing me?" they chirped, careful to keep their syntax broken enough to lead most two-leggers to underestimate them.

The fairy, who was almost as tall as Auryl, but whose slight form made them appear delicate in a way that a dragon could never be, quickly buzzed across the room and hovered in front of Auryl's shelf.

"Message for you, my liege," the fairy announced, bowing slightly.

"Go ahead," Auryl said, dropping their falsely broken Common and switching to Draconic, all while swallowing the sigh of annoyance that wanted to escape. Fairies were always so damnably formal, and Auryl did not have the patience for fairy word games today. Luckily, the message was brief.

"Your contact says that the latest attempt did not work, and that the necromancer has made a new stronghold deep in the Groffboord Mountains."

Auryl did not let any part of their thoughts show on their face as they politely dismissed the fairy messenger.

When they were alone again, with their door closed and their silencing spells in place, they cursed quietly. They couldn't help but speak their next thoughts aloud, they were so consumed with frustration.

"What are you after this time, Cousin? And how many more adventurers must I throw at you before you give up?"

More from Virginia McClain

Dungeons & Dragon Dating:
Dungeons & Dragon Dating
Hatchets & Heartache
(coming soon)
Nuptials & Necromancy
(coming soon-ish)

Chronicles of Gensokai:
Blade's Edge
Traitor's Hope
Sairō's Claw
Eredi's Gambit
(coming soon)

The Victoria Marmot series:
Victoria Marmot and the Meddling Goddess
Victoria Marmot and the Inconvenient Prophecy
Victoria Marmot and the Shadow of Death
Victoria Marmot and the Dragon's Rage
Victoria Marmot and the Road to Hell

Short Story Collections:
Rain on a Summer's Afternoon
The Alchemy of Sorrow

www.virginiamcclain.ca

Acknowledgements

ACKNOWLEDGEMENTS ARE ALWAYS a challenge for me, because my memory is awful. So if you get to the end of these acknowledgments, don't see your name, and think, "VIRGINIA how am *I* not on this list?!?" Then you probably are, in my heart, but my brain just forgot about you when I sat down to write this. Feel free to send me a message letting me know that I have failed you, and I will do my best to rectify it. Meanwhile, here are the folks this book could not have been written without, in no particular order, that my brain has not forgotten.

First up, **Bridget Broomfield (and Jeremy!)** over at Broomfield Editing. Both of whom are excellent friends, fabulous editors, and folks who were willing to put up with a ridiculously tight turn around to help me get the GenCon Edition of this book out the door between June and August of 2024. That was intense. Y'all are heroes. Also, thanks for being amazing humans who I treasure spending time with. That part didn't *directly* get this book written, but it sure helps me enjoy life enough to want to write books. Massive hugs to you both.

Next up **Pam (PS Livingstone)** for being a wonderful friend, an excellent editor, and for doing a fabulous final round of edits on this book after I realized that my rushed release in August had led to me introducing a number of errors despite the fabulous job that my first editors had done! And also for letting me crash on your couch for WorldCon, for convalescing with me afterwards, and for letting me play your PS5. You rock!

Dear reader, any errors that you find left in this text are all my own, either stubbornly kept despite being advised otherwise, or clumsily introduced as I went through tracked changes and fumbled the acceptance of my wise and worthy editors.

Next up, I need to thank **M.L. Wang** and **Intisar Khanani** for their fabulous late night cover design consults, general encouragement, and for being my bestest buds. And I'm going to go ahead and throw **Mike Shel** in here as well because he also forms part of our indefatigable GenCon Author Squad, and y'all are the best darn cheerleaders in the whole world and my favorite folks to sell books with! Thanks for all the ways you've helped me over the past few years.

And before I go any further I should probably thank **Olivia Atwater, M.D. Presley, and Tao Wong**, all of whom helped me write the blurb for this book. If you bought this book because of the back cover text (or book description on amazon) you are here because of these lovely folks who are all much better at writing blurbs than I am. Extra special thanks go to **Olivia** who took time out of her very busy schedule despite being overwhelmed with life stuff, to look at my complete wreck of a blurb and point me in the direction of the correct blurb genre.

Next up I need to thank **Tom Jilesen** for cover feedback and suggestions, **Bryce O'Connor** for title brainstorming for the series, and **Jackson Dickert** for brainstorming and moral support. Also, I want to thank all three of these fine folks for being good listeners, fellow chaos beasts, and people I will happily drop whatever I'm doing to go hang out with. Also, special thanks to **Bryce** for providing a writers retreat just when I needed one.

Of course, many thanks go, as always, to **Corey, Cedar, and Pica;** the folks who keep me going every day and who cheer me on every step of this wild book writing and publishing journey!

And along those lines many thanks go to **Anna W.** for long walks, good talks, and insisting I buy at least three boxes of this book to sell at GenCon (she was right, I sold every copy I brought). Thanks also go to **Libby** for being such a good friend (and distraction) to my kiddo. And to **Dan** for being the point parent on many occasions when our kids were playing long enough that I had time to write, edit, or format this book.

Massive thanks also go to **Johnny McDowell**, for being a truly fabulous friend, an inspiration, and someone who I can talk about anything with. For encouraging me to write this book and for hanging out with Cedar a whole bunch while I did it!

Also, many thanks go to **Diana** for helping me get enough momentum going to actually finish the final edits on this book when I was stuck in the Land of No Motivation.

Finally, massive thanks go to the **DNF Crew**, who are always the best pocket friends a lonely author could ask for, along with the **TTen Slack**, and the **SFF Twitter Discord.** So many of y'all helped me with blurb attempts, general encouragement, venting to the void, and just general camaraderie. I love that our online community of

SFF authors is so supportive, friendly, and willing to help. Y'all are the best.

Last but FAR from least, thank **YOU**, dear reader for picking up this book and giving it a shot. I hope you enjoyed it! I wouldn't still be publishing books if it weren't for folks like you. (I'd probably still be writing them and hiding them away just for myself—I'm weird like that—but I would not be going through the trouble of making them book shaped, having them edited, and getting them out where folks can see them.) I appreciate every one of you! And if you feel like leaving a review of the book anywhere, that would be massively helpful. Reviews attract new readers, and make a huge difference to small indie authors like me!

About the Author

Virginia McClain is an author who masqueraded as a language teacher for a decade or so. When she's not reading or writing she can generally be found playing outside with her four legged adventure buddy and the tiny human she helped to build from scratch. She enjoys climbing to the top of tall rocks, running through wilderness, dangling upside down from long fabric, and carrying a foldable home on her back whenever she gets a chance. She's also fond of word games, and writing descriptions of herself that are needlessly vague.

Find out more about Virginia and her books at:
www.virginiamcclain.ca

www.ingramcontent.com/pod-product-compliance
Lightning Source LLC
Chambersburg PA
CBHW061348310726
48974CB00001B/250